BORDER LESS

A LITERARY ANTHOLOGY

Borderless: A Literary Anthology
KDP edition ISBN: 9781908549648
IngramSparks edition ISBN: 9781908549655

Published by BLA & Brunel University London Press
Instagram @brunellitanthology

A catalogue record for this book is available at the British Library.

Introduction © Bernardine Evaristo 2024
Partition; *Into Blue*; *Put it on Record* © Mira Mookerjee 2024
We is bigger than We; *Sweet Buns*; *Churchlady Birds* © Emma Lindsey 2024
The Welsh Tale © Linda Swidenbank 2024
Noumenal world; *Welcome, home-seeking wanderer, to India Club*; *Afterword* © Smriti Sarma 2024
OPTION 2: THE PROLONGED CALAMITIES © Alexia Guglielmi 2024
Nature is near to ruins © Holly Grieveson 2024
EN|JA|IT - EN|IT|JA - IT|JA|EN - IT|EN|JA - IT|EN|JA - IT|JA|EN © Aisha Brown Colpani 2024
Let us be lockkeepers; *Abiding in Liminal Space*; *An un-understandable situation* © Jennie Horchover 2024
Farishta © Mahjaben Hussain 2024
Midnight Repatriation Flight © Sundus Hassan-Nooli 2024
Wings; *When India was One* © Neelam Sharma 2024
The First Time © Harshita Kaushik 2024
Overview © Jessica McCarthy 2024
A Chicken in the Oven; *13.* © Grace Amui 2024
Friday Nights at Wetherspoons: "I don't miss him" © Natasha Stewart 2024
Sometimes © Tamsyn Marie Down 2024
Eternal Sunshine © Sophie Nambufu 2024
I am the Borderless © Alex Ayling-Moores 2024
Loving at opposite ends of the day; *For Benjamin* © Helen Williams 2024
A Walking Metaphor © Damian R. Laprus 2024
The New Normal © Libby Rochester 2024
A Shoulder Like Yours; *Dear Benjamin* © Rowan Reddington 2024
Benjamin © Duncan MacDowall 2024

The authors assert their moral right to be identified as authors of this work.

This is a work of fiction. All characters, organisations, and events in this work are either products of the author's imagination or are used fictitiously.

All rights reserved. No part of this publication may be reproduced, distributed, or transmitted in any form or by any means, including photocopying, recording, or other electronic or mechanical methods, without the prior written permission of the copyright owner, except for the use of brief quotations in a book review and certain other noncommercial uses permitted by copyright law. To request permissions from the author, contact the publisher at blablabooks24@gmail.com.

Cover art and layout by Alexia Guglielmi

Dedicated to Professor Benjamin Zephaniah

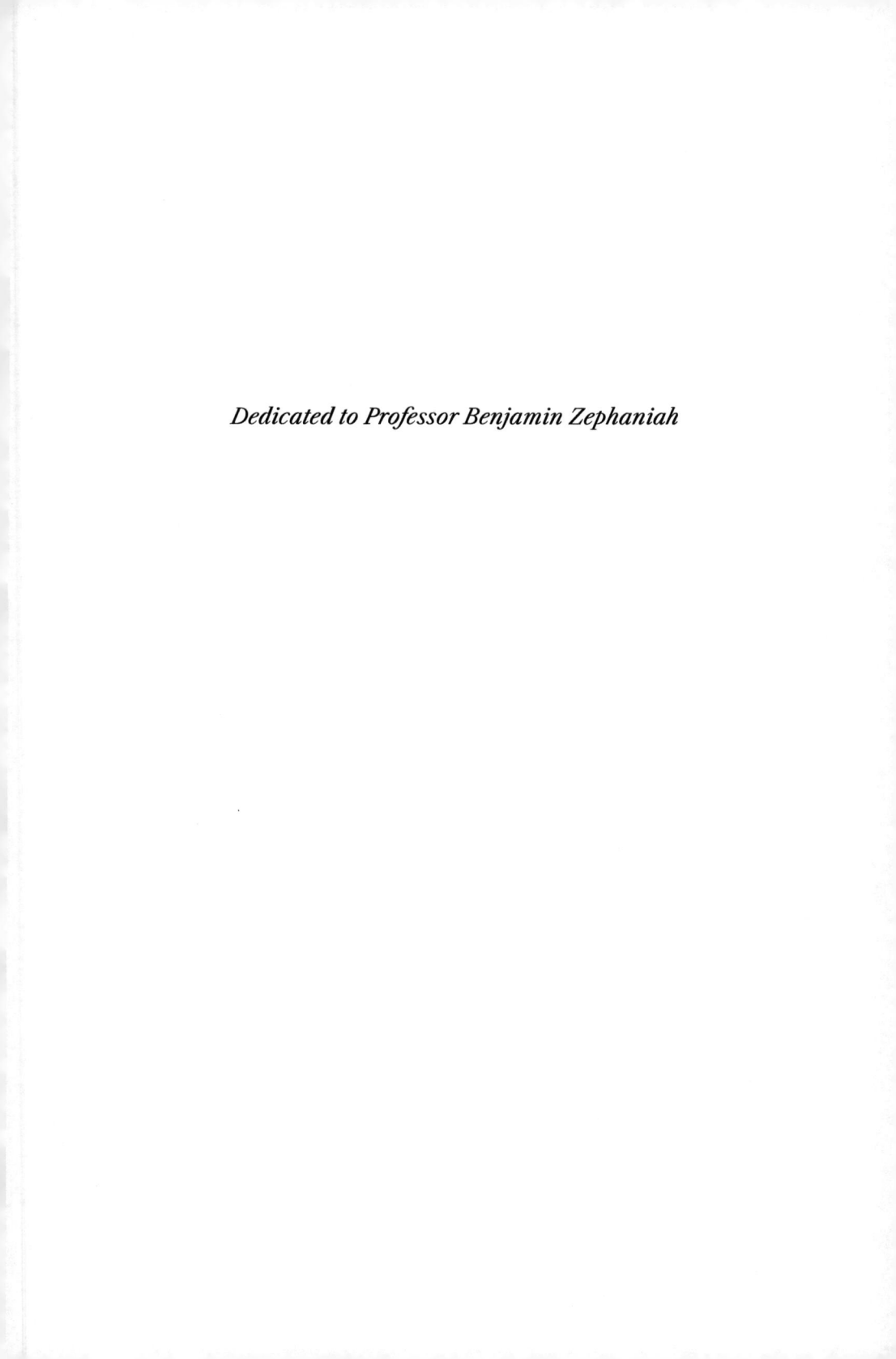

"This planet is for everyone, borders are for no one. It's all about freedom."

Benjamin Zephaniah, *Refugee Boy*

A NOTE FROM THE EDITORS

Our brainchild *Borderless* was born from the flurry of questions that come with being individuals who do not fit into, or accept, clear categorisations. The six of us studied Creative Writing at Brunel University, and our after-class discussions at café 1966 would always return to queries about language, terminology, identity and belonging. We use different ways to describe ourselves, but we all navigate multi-hyphenated identities; whether this hyphen appears between Filipino-Italian, Somali-American, British-Bangladeshi, British-Indian or Indian-English, just like so many in our generation, we know what it is like to feel that you are somewhere in-between. In-betweenness is the connective tissue that binds the works you are about to read, and through this anthology we hope to transport you to that in-between space; a space where nothing is concrete and everything is malleable, where you can feel both frightened and free, a space that allows you to regard the world from new perspectives, and recognise the strengths and constraints that finite labels can bring – a space where you are borderless.

Our much loved Creative Writing professor Benjamin Zephaniah passed away in December 2023. To Benjamin, who dedicated his life to the fight for social justice and whose work will continue to inspire people to open their minds and choose kindness, *Borderless* is for you.

From Editors Alexia Guglielmi, Sundus Hassan-Nooli, Mahjaben Hussain, Harshita Kaushik, Mira Mookerjee & Neelam Sharma.

All of BLA's profits made from Borderless *will be donated to Inquest charity, which Benjamin was a patron of. Inquest is the only charity providing expertise on state related deaths and their investigation. They lobby to ensure that government, state and corporate bodies are held to account and that action is taken in response to systemic failing. Find out more at inquest.org.uk.*

CONTENTS

Introduction
Bernardine Evaristo — 2

Partition
Mira Mookerjee — 6

We is bigger than We
Emma Lindsey — 8

The Welsh Tale
Linda Swidenbank — 10

I. Noumenal World
Smriti Sarma — 16

II. Afterword
Smriti Sarma — 20

OPTION 2: THE PROLONGED CALAMITIES
Alexia Guglielmi — 22

Nature is near to ruins
Holly Grieveson — 30

EN/JA/IT - EN/IT/JA - IT/JA/EN - IT/EN/JA - JA/IT/EN - JA/EN/IT
Aisha Brown Colpani — 32

Abiding in liminal space
Jennie Horchover — 36

Farishta
Mahjaben Hussain — 38

Midnight Repatriation Flight
Sundus Hassan-Nooli — 44

Put it on Record
Mira Mookerjee — 46

Welcome, home-seeking wanderer, to India Club.
Smriti Sarma — 48

Wings
Neelam Sharma — 50

Churchlady Birds
Emma Lindsey — 52

The First Time
Harshita Kaushik — 54

Into Blue
Mira Mookerjee — 60

When India was One
Neelam Sharma — 62

Overview
Jessica McCarthy — 68

A Chicken in the Oven
Grace Amui — 72

Friday Nights at Wetherspoons: "I don't miss him"
Natasha Stewart — 76

Sometimes
Tamsyn Marie Down — 78

Eternal Sunshine
Sophie Nambufu — 80

I am the Borderless
Alex Ayling-Moores — 82

13.
Grace Amui — 88

Loving at opposite ends of the day
Helen Williams — 90

Sweet Buns
Emma Lindsey — 92

A Walking Metaphor
Damian R. Laprus   94

An un-understandable situation
Jennie Horchover   100

The New Normal
Libby Rochester   102

Let us be lockkeepers
Jennie Horchover   104

DEDICATIONS   **106**

Dear Benjamin
Rowan Reddington   108

Benjamin
Duncan MacDowall   110

A Shoulder Like Yours
Rowan Reddington   112

For Benjamin
Helen Williams   114

List of Contributors   118

Acknowledgements   124

Introduction

Bernardine Evaristo

Borders are integral to who we are as countries, cultures, communities, as well as to the identity of individuals shaped by their relationship to sovereignty. Territorial topographical borders exist to theoretically define and demarcate, enclose and protect national and regional boundaries. The controversial issues around physical borders make headlines in the news. We read about the wars and battles, migration and immigration, and the struggles of those attempting to find their way through borders, and resistance to them doing so. There are also the metaphorical borders that might be personal, intellectual, creative or ethical, and which are no less tangible or embedded in how we live today – the distinctions and boundaries that constitute aspects of everyday life. The concept of borderlessness in this anthology is therefore fertile territory for writers with family origins all over the world, as well as in Britain, and who bring this exciting cultural cross-fertilisation to their imaginations.

Borderless showcases the wide range of the talents of Creative Writing students who have a history of producing anthologies of their work. These prove to be a record, a testament, a celebration, a collaboration, a community memory and a collective offering of their writing during their time here at Brunel University.

This book is also in memory of our Creative Writing colleague, Professor Benjamin Zephaniah, who sadly passed away in 2023. He had a remarkable career, uniquely its own, and his poetry and performances made poetry accessible to generations of people, especially the young, who might not otherwise have been drawn to it. I first saw Benjamin perform at the Albany Empire theatre in Deptford in 1982 at the start of his career and I got to know him when we both started at Brunel University at the same time, in 2011. He was someone who, during the course of his life and career, crossed many boundaries – from his difficult teenage years and time spent in Borstal, to becoming Britain's most famous poet and a household name. His writing and career spanned and fused poetry, spoken word, theatre, children's fiction, non-fiction, television presenting and other creative collaborations. His death was premature and tragic - that someone so full of energy and life, so healthy and fit, should be removed from us when he had many more years ahead of him as an important and unique voice in literature and society. I think he'd be very happy to know how much he was valued as a presence at Brunel, and that creative writing students are honouring him in this way.

Walk Soft. Walk Good.

Your amazing energy is still with us. RIP Benjamin Zephaniah 1958-2023.

Partition

Mira Mookerjee

We sit in silence, squashed in like sardines. Six to a cabin bed and more on the floor, our limbs overlapping, bodies close enough to feel the heat of each other's breath. To my right, a stranger swallows periodically, his Adam's apple bobbing with the rock of the train, while a child sitting across cries quietly into his mother's lap, his hair ruffled from her fingers running through it. I try to look into his mother's eyes, but she continues to stare out of the train window. I wonder what images she can see dancing on the glass. I want her to tell me, to take me with her – but I will not ask. Instead, I fill my lungs with the heavy air passing between us and try to calm myself, but it does not stop my mind from racing back to the bloodshed. I know the man beside me is thinking about the same thing, but we won't speak of it. We will not allow our terror to be solidified with words.

The soil outside is still soft from a heavy monsoon, but no amount of rain can wash away the new lines that have been drawn into our land. These borders, which rip through the middle of Bengal and Punjab are a leaving present from the British; the last stamp of their divide and conquer colonial tactic to ensure our countries are left weakened and easier to control from a distance – but where these lines have been drawn exactly, for us on the train, is unclear. All we have been told is that once we cross the border, we will be safe; so, we travel blindly, hoping that we will make it past an invisible line between land that looks the same on both sides.

The man beside me offers me a sweet, but my throat is too dry to eat. I take it regardless and thank him quietly.

We are lucky to be on a train, inside a carriage. Above us, people sit on the roof, and to our left and right they hang onto the frame, their arms wrapped around one another to stop them from falling. Others travel on exposed carriages designed for goods and livestock, or pile on the top of trucks and inside cars. Many, including my father and my brother, have been unable to board a train or truck and are making the journey on foot; a few precious items from home carried on their backs, my mother's mother's jewellery hidden between the folds of their clothes. The woman opposite me is clinging onto a bag of cooking equipment, a kangni wala glass, a cooking pot, a pestle and mortar. I too have my own small bag, which holds a pashmina shawl wrapped around pictures of my family. My father has told me to show the images to officials when I arrive, and that I should use the shawl as payment to help me find him. This bag is all I have from the home my family has lived in for generations. I left in a rush, my bed unmade, an open book on my pillow. I wonder how long my belongings will remain frozen like that – or if our house has already been raided, the chair where my great grandfather used to sit thrown out onto the street; the blanket made by my mother torn and muddied.

I shake the thought away and tear the soft sweet in two, placing half in my mouth and offering the other half to the crying child. He wipes his eyes and takes it, filling his cheeks with syrup. The man beside me smiles with warmth as his mother fixes her gaze on me. She nods with gratitude, but her eyes are burning like a campfire, with a mixture of love and rage only a mother knows. She looks at me deeply, drawing me in, and I feel the terror inside me subside. Her eyes are sharp, alert, and it is quickly so clear what she has been thinking – her mind has been focused on the future, and the home she will build when she arrives on the other side.

We is bigger than We

Emma Lindsey

We is bigger than We
Up through navel string: me, to you and back to Solomon
Blood lines course, crossing river beds of ancestry, where
Deep meets oceans deep
Survivors, we from Africa, Guyana, Russia to Dewsbury
Lineage bought and sold, the narrative grows, but who bought what
    and what was sold?
Stories mining Demerara gold legacies
Peculiar people, royalty, stepping free, in bondage to our ancestry

Down through navel string: bloodlines course borderless
Definitions bring renditions of our ancestry
Solomon's East African hair coils around Granny's bent little finger
Ashkenazi hook for an I, a promise to the sky
A bone to tether thread, catch and tie back to family crochet
Woven holes of negative space that hold the place
For us to grow bigger than We.

The Welsh Tale

Linda Swidenbank

Climb, she said, pulling me along, resisting my weariness, pushing the pace. At last, and past the bend, we stood in awe of the sweeping view. The ten or more miles we had walked melting behind us.

One way to England, and to the left, Wales.

She moved ahead, and after several minutes found it, a little wooden post marking the spot where Offa had brought his border of division – the Dyke, over a millennium ago. The Mercian king of the Anglo-Saxons had commanded his men to build a mud, stone, and wood border to keep the unruly Celts to the West.

We sat, legs spread in front of us, unthreading our muddy boots, spritzed from the soggy meadow we had clambered through, and all the time gazing at the view. Skylarks circled above, while a hawk swooped steadily down to a hedgerow, surveying all of the landscape in its quest for unsuspecting prey. Tufts of clumpy grass weaved over the man-made bump, etched into the land and into the distance, and all the while, the wind whistled around us.

"I think the border was planned from sea to sea, from north to south..." I said, "and strange to start it in the middle."

She nodded, her eyes still on the hawk.

"The skirmishes of resistance meant it wasn't finished. Well, not the way Offa commanded...is it any wonder the Celts are so rebellious, pushed to the craggy mountain edges, losing fertile lands like these?"

"Perhaps your dragons would breathe fire at them," she laughed.

"Spitting their fiery breath at your ancestors," I teased back.

She smiled at me, forgiving my nostalgic recall of homeland and history.

I thought about our first meeting in the Cardiff pub well over a year ago; how soon I had felt so comfortable with her, happy that friends had brought us together, seeing something in each of us that might appeal to the other. We have a friend, going to the quiz night, come along, they urged.

She unleashed any number of questions at me that evening, over the noise, in her soft west country lilt. I told her about my education research, my passion to further the historical work I loved. I told her the more you know, the more it bridges differences. She nodded, perhaps amused by my strange earnestness. I think after the fifth pint I said I would even forgive her for being English! She laughed and said how unfortunate I was 'a Welsh one' because she did quite like me, but she'd try to get over it. Welsh and English banter, that was all.

We took in our green surroundings, enjoying all that was around us.

"Not what Offa intended is it, this Welsh and English coupling?"

She smiled.

I had earmarked a pub on the map, ironically called The Prince of Wales. Known for its excellent food on the borders, but more so for its stunning riverbank views. She didn't know at this moment why, but soon she would. I'd dropped a pin to check our distance to it, and we needed to quicken our pace if we were to make it in good time. The sun, still high in the sky, would soon lower; we scrambled up, re-tied our boots and carried on at a pace.

"You know that the various so-called English 'Princes of Wales' had the castles built? Places like Harlech, Conwy and Caernarfon. The country has more castles than the entire continent of Europe! Designed to control us in our own lands. With 'princes' demanding allegiance when they came among us, even trying to stop us speaking our own language!

"Bend the will to thy sword," I shouted, in some imaginary medieval play-acting with a stick I found alongside the path.

"Very Game of Thrones," she laughed. "Your favourite pub quiz topic."

"Princes with English names like Edward, Charles, George, William, and Henry, not the true Welsh princes with names like Rhodri, Hywel Dda, Owain, Llywelyn Fawr," I said, carefully rolling my tongue to get the pronunciations right. "Born by blood and language, not by some east to west land-grab."

Of course, she wouldn't know any of this. School had indoctrinated her only about the Tudors, not the history of Wales and our point of view. Early on, after we'd been dating a few weeks, she beat me at the pub quiz, matching the right Henry to the Act of Union.

"That's the one who discarded our emblems and traditions, unlike his father I'll have you know, who appreciated us a little more, and actually liked our music and poetry and flew our dragon flag."

"Why are you so different?" she asked. "The Welsh, I mean?"

"I guess our identity has been crafted, layer upon layer, not by things, but of mood, and of rebellion against almost everything over the centuries. The stories get passed through the generations and re-enacted in places like Eisteddfod – opportunities to bring up rituals, indulge in our poetry, our lyricism, our storytelling."

"Ah, the melancholy."

"There's a word for it – hiraeth. Something untranslatable in English, but it's about our spirit, our yearning for homeland and pride, all mixed in."

I paused. Unexpectedly, a tear sprang. She laughed at my emotion.

"Come on, there's a pub in the distance. Must be the one you were telling me about."

She strode off, and I followed, and within the hour we were sitting beside the fire nook, waiting for cockles, mussels, and home-made buttered bread. In front of us, pints of Herefordshire cider glinting in the pin lights of sun streaming through the pub windows.

"I think of coal-tips and castles when I think of Wales," she said eventually.

"Another invasion..." I stated. "Economic conquerors in different centuries. Valuable grey diamond slate in the north, and seams of rich coal in the south. Both key to the industrial revolution...and all those buildings you see with the slate roofs, well it mostly came from the ground in Wales. The coal fed the engines of Victoriana, more pits, deeper to make more money, and scary places to work, dangerous, and full of dust and limited understanding of the cost to their lungs. They had Sunday off, mind, where they were expected in their finest clothes at the Methodist chapels, and preachers encouraged a different type of subservience. God would save them apparently!"

She nodded, now used to my mini lectures but looked a little relieved when the food turned up; it looked delicious in front of us. Welsh seafood fare on the English border, although I spared ordering her the seaweed laverbread, unsure why it appealed to my fellow citizens.

"I'm off to Bangor next month."

"You haven't mentioned this before?"

"I've been asked to present a paper at the University. You can come if you want to...why don't you?"

She said she'd like to, agreeing to see more of this precious Wales I keep telling her about and she hadn't been to the North.

We eagerly finished our food and cider and walked outside. I encouraged a walk toward a small path running along the river embankment, thankful to see it empty. I guided her to a tree with outstretched limbs touching the surface of the water. She perched, said it was stunning, well worth the walk. She watched as a skimming dragonfly meandered its way among the reeds. Her enthral at the nature scene allowed me to discreetly reach into my rucksack, pulling out a small ball of tissue paper, which I carefully pushed into the palm of my hand as she continued to follow the wildlife.

I kneeled, carefully avoiding a mud spot, and delicately took her hand.

"Will you marry me?"

She turned back. Gasped a little. She looked around, suspecting a camera lens to poke through the tree branches, but her eyes quickly came back to mine.

"Of course. My God – *yes*."

We quietened.

Here.

Us.

On the Welsh/English border.

It was perfect.

15

I. Noumenal World

Smriti Sarma

I will not tread the borders
between knowing and unknowing
to glimpse at promised clarity
which is not for my eyes
to see.

At the barbed wire fence
fissuring delusion
from realisation
I will hover timidly
like steam wafting
from eyes that rave
Savitrian, Orphean
in their pursuit
of nether bound dreams.

It is not advisable
they say
to stray
too far past the bounds
of one's adopted truths
Lunacy lurks

in the stars that swim
in skies other than mine.

Only the brave
or the foolish
choose to fall
between the cracks
of perception
and omniscience
all the life in the world quails
before the gravitational force
of an illusion that surpasses them
in embellished grandeur.

But Reader, if you say
I shall
Swim in the rivers
that divide the banks
of dark and baryonic matter
Plunge into its depths to look
for suns without planets
and planets without suns
Seek an audience with the Divine
particulate, indivisible
Trade my eyes
for those of a mantis shrimp
Fetch insight
like a polished pearl
from the geothermal
cradles of life.

But will it be insight enough
for you and I
to stop hesitating

to quit yearning
to cease hovering
at the border
between knowing and unknowing?

to end ventures
between boyhood
and the border
between knowing and uncertainty

II. Afterword

Smriti Sarma

After all,
after death,
all of our truths commingle
Borderless
and make for the stars
darkly energised
to rip apart
all the lies
we sustained
when alive.

OPTION 2: THE PROLONGED CALAMITIES

Alexia Guglielmi

MAY 2173

OPTION 2: HISTORIC CIVILIZATIONS: THEIR GROWTH, DEATH AND REBIRTH: 2035-2056: THE PROLONGED CALAMITIES

The extracts are transcribed from the personal journals of Penny Portdove (age: 28-33), dated between FEB 2049 - JUL 2054. Portdove lived in a Minority Higher Income Nation (MHIN) and worked as a personal assistant to John Runock (est. age: 46-51), a businessman for XYZ Ltd., the largest clothing manufacturer at the time.

Analyse the roles that power, wealth, morality and social precarity played in popular mid-C21st Western mentality, in reference to the Prolonged Calamities and as evidenced in Portdove's account.

[24 MARKS]

EXTRACT 1 – FEBRUARY 2049

Week one! Exhausted but excited. This could be incredibly rewarding, and thankfully I get along well with the other assistants. I ate lunch twice with Helena this week, who got me the interview, and tried a *[PARAGRAPH CUT FOR BREVITY.]*

John – excuse me, *Mr. Runock* – is fine, if unsympathetic. I asked him if I could work around preschool pickup hours and he's letting me take a long & late lunch, but it's only meant to be a temporary measure. He suggested I hire a nanny (he barely pays me living standard), or ask my mother to help with childcare. He knows she lives in a different city – I remember telling him on my first day as he mentioned being born there...

Fine, John's an arse. But I'll endure it. The career progression path is good enough that I'll smile through gritted teeth. I had a moment of doubt when an old uni friend messaged me after announcing my new role on LinkedIn[1]. Pointed out the company was involved in a pollution scandal a few years ago and accused me of selling my soul. I looked it up. They paid a settlement fee and have committed to a reduced environmental impact plan that they aim to complete in twelve year's time.

It wouldn't have changed my mind either way. Livvy is only four but I'm already worried about the future, and Mum shouldn't have to work forever either.

This is worth it. It will be worth it.

---

[1] A business-oriented social media platform

EXTRACT 2 – FEBRUARY 2051

[...] Liv opened the biscuit jar without my help today and I almost burst into tears. I swear she's growing up while I'm looking the other way, chasing after John in the office, chasing after hundreds of lost hours of sleep at home. I'm missing her so much even when I'm right next to her that I took her for a walk this weekend, just to hold her hand for an hour straight.

It's the coldest it's been in weeks. The sleeves on her jacket were too short, exposing her wrists to the frigid air. The entire time I had to reassure myself that nobody can be the perfect parent, let alone me. <u>Thank god Mum helps when she can.</u>[2]

Liv and I ended up at the park. We sat by a heat lamp with a hot chocolate to share, which she almost dropped when she pointed at a hedgehog sniffing around the base of a tree. She begged me to take it home in between snot-filled sobs. I had to drag her away kicking and screaming, which triggered her asthma. I was so worried I dropped her inhaler. She dropped the hot chocolate.

We got home and I managed to put her to bed by the time Mum returned from her shift at the store. I told her about Liv's asthma and the hedgehog. Mum mentioned they're hibernating creatures – if it was outside it must have been foraging for food, tricked by last week's warm spell.

While she hopped in the shower I looked up their diet – worms and bugs – and thought about how it's been so cold lately that even the soil has been frozen.

The hedgehog will go hungry.

I don't know what came over me. I checked on Liv before making my way back to the park. I found the tree where we'd seen the hedgehog and searched it for at least twenty minutes before the foolishness of it all hit me. I wasn't dressed properly for the outside;

---

[2] Entry from a few weeks prior states Portdove's mother moved into their flat and "sleeps on the sofa, works evenings at a supermarket down the road."

my fingers were numb and unresponsive from the cold. I was shivering in such uncontrollable bouts that I nearly bit my tongue off.

I decided to run back home to warm myself up but slipped on a patch of ice. Bruised my knees and cut my palm open on a rock. Luckily Mum was asleep by the time I was back, so no questions asked.

I might have sprained my wrist.

Will get it checked tomorrow.

EXTRACT 3 – JANUARY 2054

Runock's responsible for the new production plant they're setting up in Vietnam[3] and wants me to fly there as his representative. As if the pollution cloud hasn't grown big enough. I'll have to face the workers and act like their human rights aren't being infringed.

Yesterday I threatened to quit if he sent me and today he gave me a raise large enough to shut me up. God, my hand is shaking as I write. It's enough for Mum to quit her job. Enough to think about buying a house. Enough to retire in a few years and dedicate all my time to Liv and send her off to uni without batting an eye. It's what I've been waiting for since the moment I took the job.

But Runock made the conditions of the raise very clear. XYZ can't afford another whistleblower, especially with the second pollution scandal so recent in everyone's minds...

I never thought I'd put a price on my conscience.

Sometimes I wonder about that old uni friend who warned me about the company...what words would she have for me now?

---

[3] Majority Lower Income Nation (MLIN)

EXTRACT 4 – MAY 2054

Liv was sick today. Normally it's not an issue but Mum couldn't get out of her shift. They threatened to fire her if she didn't show, which I doubt is legal but frankly don't have the time to chase. Despite my raise she doesn't want to risk it. Luckily, I was able to arrange WFH[4] to look after Liv.

She's been poorly a lot recently. GP[5] said it's expected given her asthma and worsening air conditions, so not to worry – "She'll improve as the air does." I had to fight the urge to slap him. She's been off enough from school she might need to redo the year. We shouldn't have to wait around for the air to clear for her health to get better.

The day only worsened with the arrival of a tropical thunderstorm, of all things. Liv is still scared of thunder and spent the entire afternoon in tears. Clearly the leviathan fans the government erected two years ago are a fucking joke. If this were a sitcom I'd be howling. *"Fans to blow away the pollution? We live on a fucking globe! Where would it go? And what does the wind know about borders?"*

Apparently what the fans *have* managed to achieve is fuck with the ocean currents and definitively ruin its wildlife. Saw it on the news this morning. Liv won't be able to have her birthday salmon bake anymore. As it's still five months away I'm hoping she has enough time to adjust to the disappointment.

---

[4] acronym for *work from home*, an arrangement wherein an office employee could perform their job remotely

[5] acronym for *General Practitioner*

EXTRACT 5 – JULY 2054
[TRANSCRIBER'S NOTE: THIS PAGE WAS WRITTEN ON SCRAP PAPER AND INSERTED INTO PORTDOVE'S JOURNAL]

Contacted SONS & SONS re: their services. Traditional is £6,803. Includes body collection, urn, cremation service, funeral conductor. Enquired if urn can be printed with Olivia's name – yes, with additional fee.
+ £790 church
+ £? flower displays
+ £? catering
+ £? memorial service
+ ?

XYZ offering five days bereavement leave, up from the usual three.

YOU MAY BEGIN YOUR RESPONSE TO THIS TASK OVERLEAF

Nature is near to ruins

Holly Grieveson

I wonder how people
can walk barefoot,
treading on cigarette butts
near where they left their
highly flammable canvas shoes.
People have coughing issues,
yet choke themselves
with monoxide we produce.
We take those cigarettes,
flick them into
a graffitied alleyway,
where a gouged car
lays unconscious,
missing one of its limbs.
We're unable to take care
of the manmade, so do
Mother Nature's creations have a place?

We as humans became
so reckless, to clog up what was
a cornflower blue ceiling,
that sheltered the tickle of grass strands

beneath our feet. I long for the
freshness of the citrus fruits,
that once were born
from thriving trees.
We now stand on their graves,
concrete slabs with lichens
as the countryside's churchyard.
A pavement littered with
glass shards, where plants would be.
What can protect nature
from human behaviour?

We were designed to take care of
what was around us.
The lilies we stomped and spat on.
The leaves now wither and cry.
Is this what we think of Eden?

EN/JA/IT - EN/IT/JA - IT/JA/EN - IT/EN/JA - JA/IT/EN - JA/EN/IT

Aisha Brown Colpani

I wear my borders like a gold necklace tucked under my t-shirt. Precious but concealed. Kept just for me, but waiting, dormant, to be shown off when needed.

The stamp of my dad's DNA and the DNA of his mum and dad and – I guess – their mothers, and their fathers, is more obvious. They're the things people see first; my skin's pigment, the shape of my nose, the tight loops of my hair.

My mum is somewhere in there too, though. In certain lights, I see her side quietly existing on my face. But I don't know if I only see it because I know it's there.

Would a stranger see the outline of my mother, my grandmother – *nonna* – and grandfather – *nonno*?

I balance on these two tectonic plates, looking so much like one place that the other seems to shrink.

My pride for this blood inheritance sometimes feels misplaced; my mum was born over *there*, and my dad over *there* but what did I have to do with that? My real life has always been here. London.

They loom large though, the shadows of the two countries that made me. They are more than the earth crunching beneath my feet as I step off a plane that has crossed the English Channel or the North Atlantic to reach them. In my mind they are a patchwork; made up as much from what I'd heard in school, from mates, from crushes, TV, music, as they are the things I myself have seen and lived in each of those places.

After a teenage argument in which I lose my temper, a boy I like says to me, "That's your black side coming out." His voice is soft and laughing and maybe I laugh too. But I keep that comment, storing it where it can still be found 15 years later.

My grandma, my father's mother, sometimes translates her country's words for me, as if they hadn't taken root and flowered in the language of this city. "Bredrin" equals "friend". I know. "Yard" equals "house". *I know.*

More recently, in a city half an hour away from the town in which my mum grew up, I'm on a night out with a friend and her friends – unfamiliar faces, contrasting mine. "How do you two know each other?" Their question is one built on others, unspoken. But there's sense to their curiosity, so there I am at a picnic table under the black tent of the night sky, explaining how our two lives converge. Giving context to my friendship with this girl I've known my whole life. Then my friend announces, "Yeah you're Jamaican, and you're Italian, but most of all you're English."

And so I'm transported back into that in-between space, hovering one second over one country, the other, the other, the other still, the other. My borders don't mesh necessarily but the countries layer like the elements of a three-piece instrumental – England often the loudest.

I figure my friend's conclusion is born of the obvious things: my reticence, maybe, and how I tell jokes without laughing or even smiling. It could be that I seem too uptight, that I say "thank you" and "sorry" in places where no-one requests or expects those words. A politeness found restrictive when taken out of its house. I think she's partially right, though. London is where I feel most at home – if not completely.

But I'm not English – I'm British. Threads of Jamaica and Italy weaving my exterior. All three countries mixing, like oil and water, in my interior.

Abiding in liminal space

Jennie Horchover

I am drawn to the liminal
the thin places and times
where the physical and supernatural temporarily meet
the borders between life and death

To shorelines
wilderness
oak trees
dawn and dusk

To ancient monuments
misty weather
sacred ground
samhain and midsummers eve

Times and places as portals
finding the silence in the space in-between
living life on the threshold
here but not fully present
like the moment between dreaming and wakefulness
betwixt and between

Searching for the enchanted
connecting to the beyond
feeling the energy
abiding in liminal space

Farishta

Mahjaben Hussain

The smallest coffins are the heaviest. The people of Pakistan express their fury and grief over the small coffin, chanting in front of the Police Station.

"Justice for Neha! Justice for Neha!" in the air like a mantra.

Both men and women cry for another young life lost due to negligence and cowardice. They push against the iron gate, demanding attention. Smashing windows of police vehicles using anything they can pick up off the ground. The intense heat of a spring day heavy on their backs, sweat streaming down their foreheads.

Irene, dressed in a crimson kameez and a matching hijab, black strands of her hair peeking out, stands behind the lamppost farthest from the chaos. The disorder descends into a horrific display of policemen using batons to strike the very people they are meant to safeguard. Wails resonate in the air as Irene retreats from the sickening sound of hitting flesh. The distant cries cling to her, trailing behind like eerie whispers.

Eventually, she arrives at a house and retrieves the key from her pocket to open the door. Incoherent voices coming from the living room sound alarmed. Irene enters with quiet precision. Inside, her friend, Iqra, sits on the sofa, her eyes glued to the TV. The screen captures the bodies tightly packed together and law enforcement viciously shoving the crowd away from the gates.

"Oh, Irene? I didn't hear you come in." A soft voice calls.

Irene faces Iqra, whose eyes are burdened with black bags of distress. Her wrinkled cheek bearing trails of dried tears, her skin red and blotchy.

"Sorry," said Irene, her hazel eyes on the screen. "Your husband is out there, isn't he?"

Iqra's breath hitches, her attention falling on the TV. "Yeah. I can't believe it happened *again*. It hasn't been long since we lost—" Iqra cuts herself off.

Irene joins her friend in the living room and gently wipes away a tear from Iqra's cheek.

"It just never ends." Iqra's shoulders slump.

"What happened?" Irene asks softly.

Iqra takes the remote from the coffee table and turns off the TV. The cries disappear into a black screen.

"It's been going on for two years now. Little girls suddenly go missing. No matter how many times people tell the police, they do nothing. A few days later, the child's body turns up somewhere. Unrecognisable." She sighs. "I remember similar stories happening when my great-grandmother was alive. Children scared of leaving their homes because they believed the Boogeyman would take them away. But one day, the rumours said that a Farishta had come and killed it."

Irene arches her brow.

"Anyway, let's not talk about that. I promised we would go out for a walk together. Let me get ready and we can go."

Irene's lips curl into a small smile as she watches Iqra step into another room. Pushing herself off the sofa, Irene retreats up the stairs, passing by some family photos of three smiling faces from a time long gone now. The wooden panels creak under her feet as she climbs up the stairs to the next floor. She pushes open the door leading into a simple room with blue painted walls. In the corner sits a small bed with a mosquito net fastened to a hook above it.

She notices the full-length mirror next to the wardrobe and begins to tug gently at the hem of her kameez. Irene winces as she lifts her clothing, exposing a bloodied bandage wrapped tightly around her waist. With a gentle touch, she runs her fingertips over the material before slowly peeling off the sticky red bandage. Smooth, healed skin lies underneath; no sign of a jagged white scar. A knock abruptly echoes from the other side of the door.

"Irene?"

She shoves her kameez top down and scrunches the bandage into her fist. "Yes?"

"Come down when you're ready, OK?"

"Alright."

Irene tosses the bandage into a bin. Next, she retrieves a box of matchsticks from her pocket and strikes one against the box's edge. A flame flickers to life, the heat rolling over her face in light waves. Irene drops the match into the bin and flames engulf the bandage. It curls into itself before disintegrating into nothing. Soon, the flame's wild flickers shrink under her gaze until its form is no more.

Irene exits the room as muffled voices come from the main entrance.

"Are you hurt?" asks Iqra, urgently.

"I'm fine," a man grunts.

"But you're bleeding."

Irene quietly descends the stairs and leans against the wall, peeking at Iqra and her husband, Zahid. He covers his forehead with his hand, attempting to conceal the traces of blood from his wife. His white shirt appears ravaged by dust, torn and stretched, as if having just escaped from a brawl.

"I told you this would happen. Let me see—"

Zahid swats her hand away. "Why wouldn't I go? After what happened to Anaya, *we* had every right to be there!"

Tears appear at the corner of Iqra's eyes. Zahid's gaze softens, the hard lines of tension disappearing from his face.

"I'm sorry. There's just...a lot on my mind." He spots Irene eavesdropping and clears his throat. "Get some fresh air with Irene. You haven't gone out in a long time."

"But—"

"No buts, I'll see you later."

Zahid trudges into the house, nodding at Irene before heading upstairs. Irene turns back to Iqra, a sad smile on the woman's lips.

"Come. Let's go."

Together, they exit into the blaring sun. Strolling through town, passing the market beginning to bustle with activity; people selling spices, dates, even clothing and jewellery. In spite of the busy surroundings, they choose to enjoy a comfortable silence.

A large building echoes with laughter as boys and girls burst out, their faces joyful as they sprint towards the adults gathered outside the gate. Iqra lets out a choked whimper, but regains her composure quickly.

"She would've been running out of there by now...into my arms. Sometimes when she had full marks on a test, she would beg me for gulab jamun as a treat." Iqra lightly laughs to herself. Her bottom lip trembles at the memory, and Irene soothingly strokes her shoulder. "I'm sorry."

Iqra tears her gaze away from the children and rushes back the way they came.

Irene remains rooted to the spot as Iqra disappears around the corner. She reverts her attention to the school, her sharp eyes sweeping through the crowd. Their heartbeats blending into an erratic symphony. But a particular beat catches her attention. The calm rhythm is a striking contradiction to the chaos surrounding it. And a shadow vanishes from her line of sight.

***

Heavy footsteps thud against the dirt path while a little girl thrashes in the man's arms. Her screams are silenced by a hand clamped over her mouth. Under the watch of lampposts and the faint buzzing of mosquitoes, he forcefully drags her through the night. They enter an open garbage disposal site completely barren of people. The man drops the girl on the ground, her little body on top of a pile of rubbish. She tries to yell for help, but his hand wraps around her fragile neck. A controlled yet crazed expression plagues the man's eyes. He reaches for the hem of her dress.

A haunting whistle reverberates through the air, and the hairs on the back of his neck stand on end, stopping him. A tune so poignant and eerie it sends shivers down his spine. Draped in a long dark coat, face concealed by a black mask embellished with silver threads forming the likeness of a sinister being.

The man shoots to his feet. "What the hell is this?!" he demands, staggering backwards, nearly stepping on the little girl.

Wide innocent eyes stare up at the masked stranger who holds up a finger to their lips before waving a hand in dismissal. Stumbling to her feet, the girl flees. Step by step, the man retreats until the sight of the monstrous mask makes his knees buckle and he crumples to the ground. A gloved hand seizes the man's shirt and yanks him effortlessly into the air. The gaze of demonic red eyes meets his, penetrating his soul. His instinctual need to escape has him squirming desperately for help.

But no one comes.

The stranger opens their mouth, exposing sharp fangs craving for a taste.

"N-no! Please!"

Silencing his plea, the stranger sinks their teeth into the man's neck. Struggling to break free, he helplessly witnesses his energy drain, until there is nothing left to give.

The motionless weight falls to the ground, and Irene removes the mask from her face. As she looms over the corpse, drops of crimson flow down her chin and onto her clothes.

Farishta has eaten the Boogeyman.

Midnight Repatriation Flight

Sundus Hassan-Nooli

What will you do now that the war has ended?
Time still remains fractured and you can't recall
The fake name you gave calamity
The first time it came knocking at your door—

Hello.

It's your neighbour who knows
What your husband did during the war.

A shame neither of you can recognise his daughter.

Skilled in stomaching the dark blood that follows you.
Mercurially you revel in the comfort of death's gaze.
Because if anyone tried you know the art of how to haphazardly kill.
You're saving this skill in case the closet isn't big enough
For you and your queer children.

Knock-knock

You're doused in the scent of no return.
Can you keep hiding the graveyards in your mind?

Often you look up and lock eyes with toy soldiers.
And you never know who's more sinful.
Soon you're met with, "ma'am come with us now."

Cautionary tales borne from your madness.
Keep you tied as the world keeps turning left.

Put it on Record

Mira Mookerjee

It wasn't always like this. Grandma remembers a time before the UN's partition plan, before the war and occupation, before identity cards and borders; a time before our land was split by two names and all its histories were stitched into a single narrative. She remembers what it was like to be able to sleep through the night.

Me? I do not. I know war, bombs, raids, and destruction. I know rubble, gunshots, and hunger – but I also know grandma; I know sweet sage tea, our donkey Mufeed, and the call of the cockerel at sunrise, and I know my mum. I know her favourite blue hijab, her wise eyes, and the warmth of her skin. I do not know my father, but I know he was not a good man.

Once, Grandma mentioned that he was part of the Israeli army, but Mum said he was a Palestinian officer. I remember overhearing Grandma talking to Mum about it, but she just said that *this is Palestine, and he was an officer*, and refused to say anymore.

In our bedroom, there's a picture of three men hanging on the wall. When I was little, my mum said that the man in the middle was my father. I did not like the look of him, with his sunken eyes and his slim boyish arms holding a gun high on his shoulder, but I needed to know more.

I've tried talking to her about it now that I'm older, but she denies ever saying anything. Still, I remember what she said – so, one night, after she had gone to bed, I asked Grandma.

"Is it him? The man in the picture?" I said. "Is he my father?"

At first, she looked away, but then she shook her head.

"He was your mother's childhood sweetheart," she replied. "He is long dead now; he was not your father."

My palms felt wet with sweat, my stomach churned and I felt blood rush through my chest.

"If he isn't, then who is?" I shouted at her. "And how can I know who I am, and if I am good or bad if I do not know who my father is?"

Grandma looked at me silently for a long time until all my rage evaporated, and I was left with nothing but shame. I never shout at Grandma. I thought she would scold me, but instead, she held out her arms and nestled me into her lap.

"My child," she whispered in my ear, "your fathers are Bedouins, Assyrians, Babylonians and Persians. You are Greek, you are Roman. Your ancestors are Fatimids, Seljuks, Turks and Crusaders. They are the invaded and invaders. You are a Levantine, a Mesopotamian, an Egyptian, a Mameluke. Your ancestors are Crimean, they are Russian, Ukrainian, and Lithuanian. You come from slaves and enslavers, victims and perpetrators. You are Muslim, Jewish, Christian, and pagan; you are a Palestinian, an Arab; a combination. Your family is this land that has birthed you, and it is this holy land, this promised land, whose earth bleeds the same blood that flows so peacefully through you. You, Amina, are my world, my girl of only thirteen. How could you ever be bad, my child? How could you ever be bad?"

Welcome, home-seeking wanderer, to India Club.

Smriti Sarma

Once upon a storied century
a golden bird nesting in the world's heart
was displaced by Palash flames
and even before the smoke had settled
it was clear that nothing would ever be the same.

The ashes that still billow across the oceans
of civilisations long healed have ferried me here
a promise that existed, for years
only in the shape of words and the shingle-smooth
texture of language upon my tongue.

Raindrops twinkle on black asphalt
nature's delicate footfalls
as The Strand that bound me to monsoon
nature's unleashed might
unravels home in my soul's
soul gushing forth to dissolve
into the London downpour.

From this mist of emotion ineffable

in English and Hindi spirits emerge
floating light as baya weavers or goldfinches
hatched from the golden bird's hope flourishing
in the seventy-seventh season of freedom and rebirth.

I follow them into a thriving cultural potpourri
awash with the swaras of melt-in-mouth English vowels
elevated by the sombre intonation of a harmonium
crispy sambar-doused dosas washed down with Camden pale ale.

Here, under their angelic auspices
Besant, Russell, Nehru, Menon: the coalition
against colonialism Sarojini Naidu's ancient rage
is conquered a million times over with love.
Here, where the children of empire gather
Percy Shelley's glorious people blaze lightning
bright against the coruscating chandeliers.

Free to bear witness and free to write
amid the redolence of steaming cups of chai
and the fine spritz of grey spring from the bay windows
the avian flutter in my heart steadies
into wingbeats that soar joyously
to open, once and for all, the borders
between the east and west halves of my heart.

Wings

Neelam Sharma

I'm safe and sheltered out of the douse drizzle
but as I stare at the darting blue tits
the squawking lime green parakeets
and levitating smoky gulls
I know I'll take the leap –
test the wings that arrived
miraculous after years of wishing, dreaming
am I still human or completely bird?
I flutter and rise, the easiest
thing in the world
to float, a little more energy
beating until I've pulsed off
hovering next to charcoal branches
leaves sodden and shiny
feathers rustling as I thrust out
searching, gliding, absorbing air
rain slipping from my glossy body
the rush of momentum, speeding past
empty playgrounds, crumbling graveyards, slick rooftops
over patchwork fields and juvenile coppices
streams riffling and pulling into rivers, weaving
towards oceans that fill the horizon

a bird's eye view of scrubby hills and striated munros
bursts of fog as I surge through clouds then pure light—
I see everything
Untethered.

Churchlady Birds

Emma Lindsey

Jamaican Churchlady birds swoop out from open doors, crest the hill, then stream amid
tropical green in bright plumage of shiny yellow, red, satin-purple and black.
Umbrellas like outstretched wings keep off the bites of afternoon sun.
Bibles worn slick as silk, tucked up tight under steely arms,
On care-worn feet they step lightly, no less, in pinching Sunday shoes toward
pots of rice'n peas, stew chicken and curry goat, cooked before the yolk of morning first cracked and spilled.

Churchlady birds, hatted and starch-pressed into cornerstones, bearing generational loads.
Embracing burdens, spanning continents. Prayer the rope that binds.
Churchlady birds return chattering to their Orange Bay nests, put away their best and soon, radio worship songs rise from the bush, like frankincense, to sweet-Jesus the blessed afternoon.

The First Time

Harshita Kaushik

When Vijay told Devi he's leaving her for another woman, Devi assumed that the usual, gorgeous twenty-year-old gold digger in her prime had managed to ensnare him using her sexiness and charm. Surprisingly, she turned out to be a woman her age. Old. Neither was her husband a handsome hunk who possessed gold. He was just a local bank's branch manager.

Usually it's people in their twenties who stress about whether their partner would leave them for someone better, but as people get older, they tend to accept their partner as they are, embracing even their most annoying habits, as familiarity becomes comforting. They accept that this is their person until death.

At least that is what Devi thought.

When she was fifty, she'd looked forward to her retirement as a government school teacher in Jaipur. She'd thought when she would be sixty, she would spend all her time with her husband, making him his favourite dishes and watching old Bollywood movies together, visiting their daughter once in three months in London.

Until her husband left her and all her dreams came crumbling down.

Devi and her husband had an arranged marriage thirty-four years ago; of all the pictures that were shown to her of different men, Vijay had looked the best. White long-sleeved shirt rolled up just enough to show his gold Timex watch, his face resting on his hand. He had an ear-to-ear grin, revealing his set of perfectly aligned teeth. He had dark brown silky hair that partially covered his forehead. She had instantly fallen for him.

And he had chosen her back! Not that she did not expect it. Devi was beautiful too. A slightly plump figure, she barely touched five feet four inches, good enough for an Indian woman. However, she fetched most of her compliments for her long, thick black hair which fell right above her hips. "Compensates for her slightly dull complexion well", she'd heard the aunties in her neighbourhood say to her mother on numerous occasions.

Those thirty-four years of her marriage were as good as an Indian arranged marriage could be. They both fell in love within a few months of getting married and worked together to build a life for themselves. A good enough one.

Vijay was overall a pleasant man. Definitely one of the better ones she saw around her. First, he did not abuse her. Secondly, when her mother-in-law objected to her working to make money, he took her side. He wouldn't do extraordinary things for her, no surprises, no gifts unless she asked for one, but he respected and loved her.

Nisha came into their lives after trying for a year and then everything became about her. They were delighted to revolve their lives around her. Wasn't that what good parents did?

They fought like everyone else but in the last four years of their marriage, it seemed like whatever Devi did was wrong. Then in the last two years it felt like Vijay had given up on her. He'd become distant. She would hear his voice only when it was with Nisha or when he was on a call. He gradually stopped looking her in the eyes.

Devi tried to understand what it was that she was doing wrong. She urged Vijay to talk to her and then, finally, he talked. He was in love with someone else. Someone who he wanted to spend the rest of his life with.

Nisha was in London when Devi broke the news to her. Helpless because she couldn't leave her job and come back. Devi understood that so she never asked her to.

Devi still had her job, her school to go to. For the first time in her life she dreaded going back home. There was no home left. Now that she was sixty, there was no school to go to as well.

"You need to get out of that house," her daughter suggested to her a week after her retirement.

"Where can I possibly go? I don't know any other place. Haven't known it ever."

"Come to Lond–"

"Absolutely not. Jaipur has always been my home and it always will be."

She walked to her balcony. It was seven in the evening and the sun had just set. It was getting darker. She saw some children playing in the playground of her apartment complex. She recognised each and every one of their faces but had no idea what their names were.

She turned to look back at her home. Vijay would come back from work and sit on the couch in the living room for hours watching television. The table kept in front of it was the first expensive purchase of theirs two years after Nisha was born. The dressing table kept in the room to which the balcony she was standing in was attached was as old as their marriage. Yet they held no meaning for her anymore.

She couldn't feel more alienated from a place, could she?

A month later, Devi was in London. She had almost forgotten what it was like to live with her own daughter. How many years had they been separated? Seven? Eight?

No doubt, the city was exquisite. It had the most beautiful sky Devi had ever seen; people who were exceptionally talented and passionate; weather that would go through four seasons a day.

"Ma, I think you should join this book club that my colleague's mother goes to. You'll meet a lot of people there. You need to move on. Find joy," Nisha suggested one day.

"Nobody finds joy at my age, especially when your husband does not find you worthy enough of himself after thirty-four years."

Because all you did was worship him. When did you last think about yourself?" Nisha nearly screamed. Composing herself, she said, "That's it, I'm telling my colleague that you're interested. You can leave after a month if you don't like it."

Next Saturday afternoon, Devi found herself amongst twelve unfamiliar faces. She tried to feign calmness and composure, but inside she was trembling. Her heart was plummeting with every single beat and her breath was pacing faster. It was like she was back at school on her first day.

"You alright there?" She heard a man speaking to her.

She turned to her left and found a pair of gleaming, blue eyes blazing at her dark brown ones.

"Yes," she managed to let the words out of her mouth.

She tried to figure out his ethnicity.

"I'm David," he was beaming. *Clearly a British.*

"Devi."

"First day, huh?"

She nodded.

"What do you read?"

"I don't."

He looked at her perplexed.

"My daughter asked me to join."

"I see, here to meet new people?"

"I don't know."

"You... you new here?"

"Yeah, it's been four weeks."

"Would you fancy going for coffee?"

"Right now?"

"Yeah."

"It hasn't even started yet."

"You're clearly not here for books. It's kind of obvious why you're here. Broken marriage, right?"

"How did you know?"

"Most people are here to meet someone new, make friends. I'm also here for the same reason. I already teach literature in this school nearby. Come, let's go."

To Devi's surprise, she found herself following after him. She felt a weird kind sensation in her gut. It had been so long since she had been excited for something.

Every Saturday afternoon, Devi would leave for the club but would end up joining David in different cafes and bakeries.

He was much taller than her ex-husband was. Contrary to Vijay, he had light brown hair of which not much was left. He was kind, much kinder than Vijay ever was. He would hold doors open for her, treat her to his favourite milk cakes and hot chocolate. He even got flowers for her one day.

"These reminded me of you," he said, handing her a bouquet of white jasmine. "You smell like them."

She was dumbfounded. Vijay had never noticed her favourite scent. Devi was falling again.

"You want to join me for dinner at my place this Saturday?" He asked her when they were talking on the phone a month later.

"I can't do dinners. I haven't told Nisha about our friendship."

"What about lunch?"

Lunch it was.

He had a small two-bedroom apartment twenty minutes away from Nisha's house. It was neat and tidy, except for a few things here and there just enough to show that someone actually lived there.

"You have kids?" Devi asked.

"Three of them. Youngest one is in college and two of them are working," he said while heating up the lunch.

"What about your wife?" She hesitantly asked.

"Died, ten years ago. Breast cancer. Here," he handed her the plate on the couch. "This chicken is my speciality."

She sensed his eyes on her while she was eating.

"You're so beautiful, my god," he said.

Beautiful? Her?

She smiled at him and continued eating. "You don't look too bad yourself."

"Really? I never realised that. Thank you." They both chuckled.

"You do realise that's why I asked you for coffee, right? Please don't tell me you thought we were just going to be friends."

"I was hoping not."

He looked at her in surprise. "I'm glad. May I kiss you?"

Kiss? Did people of her age kiss? How was she supposed to react? She definitely did not want to say no.

His lips were gentle and Devi was struggling to keep up with his movement. He gradually went down her neck, kissing it softly, almost with caution. My god it felt so good. So, so good.

She had had sex, obviously, but she had never made love. Was this how sex was supposed to feel?

David caressed her breasts and abdomen, kissing all of her body.

"You are really beautiful, you know?"

No she didn't.

She did not want it to end. It was weird how comfortable she felt, as if she *belonged* there, with him.

She then went to the bathroom to take a shower and looked at herself in the mirror.

She actually was beautiful. So beautiful. She only wasn't reminded of it enough.

Into Blue

Mira Mookerjee

In this room our eyes are fishing boats
Drifting out over the ocean
Unanchored, unmoored,
Their oars rising through the water
As waves rock the bow

The sky slips into the horizon
As we sink into the sea
Unlimited, unconfined,
Our palms clasped like closed shells
And legs tangled into mangrove roots

What use are words here?
When the sound of your breath says enough,
When in the air dawn is breaking
And your eyes hold an island, an oasis, the sun.

Outside, the rain falls pitta patta on the windowpane,
Rivers spilling down the glass,
Water meeting sand again,
Pulling us back to shore.

When India was One

Neelam Sharma

When I was a child, we lived in a village called Bhatwara in the Chamba region. Daniyah's family moved into the house across the road from us when I was seven and she was eight. I remember watching shyly as the tall girl with silky hair flowing down her back clambered off the cart with her older teenage sister. Her mother wore a dusky pink scarf thrown loose over her kohl black hair and carried a baby wrapped in a blue blanket. She smiled at me and told her youngest daughter to say hello to the welcoming committee. Dani bounded over with her big-toothed grin. We were friends from that moment onward. We played in each other's yards, collected eggs from Mother's chickens, climbed trees to reach guavas, savoured the fragrant ripening fruit, crunching the creamy seeds. We walked to and from school together, making a twenty-minute journey home stretch into an hour and a half as we thought of one last thing we must tell the other before we said bye. We even wrote to each other using code, to share secrets about favourite teachers and school crushes without her nosy older sister Manika finding out.

Their baby brother Zubin was a chubby cheeked cherub who babbled away happily, who grabbed my finger as if he had something vital to relay. Manika often looked after him, but he was entranced by Dani. I wished I had a sibling who adored me that way. As he started to walk, he would follow her around trying to join in with our play.

One evening we were organising a game of hide and seek with a group of local children, deciding if the seeker would count to 50 or 100 when we heard shouts and religious chanting. There was something ragged and angry about the voices. We looked at each other; this wasn't a routine call to prayer or festive celebration. Mother was hanging out the washing and she stopped, dropping a white shirt onto the dirt. She ran over to us, grabbed my hand, instructed the other children to go home now.

"What is it, Mata?" I asked.

"Some people are angry," her voice shook, and her grip tightened as she pulled me inside.

"What about?"

The chants continued into the evening and the following day. Our parents told us to come straight home from school today, no loitering. On our way we were stopped by two men wearing topis on their heads; they asked Dani if I was Muslim. Dani told them we were sisters. She pointed at the house closest to us and claimed that we lived there before rushing us into its backyard. We waited behind a bin until an Ayah came out to throw something away. It scared her seeing us crouched in the shadows.

"What are you doing?" she demanded.

"Sorry, sorry. There were men on the road asking us about our religion," Dani implored.

She asked our names and knew where we lived.

"Ok, wait," she said, and came back with the father of the house, a tall upright man with slicked back hair, carrying a stick. He took us home walking so quick, we had to run to keep up. I remember thinking he didn't need a walking stick. We watched as he spoke to Dani's Mum, who shook her head, twisting the corner of her headdress between her hands.

"From now on, we take you to school and pick you up," she told us after he headed back down the road swinging the stick around in front of him.

That night we smelt the burning of a bonfire, saw flames blazing into the night. Bits of flickering paper, like fireflies, lifted into the air, the warm breeze carrying them and dropping charred fragments into yards. The smell of smoke coated the air and the clothes forgotten outside on the line.

There were huddled conversations with relatives, friends and neighbours who hushed when we entered. We no longer listened to mystery stories on the radio in the evenings; it was now turned to the news the whole time. Mother and Father strained to hear the broadcasts and hurried to switch them off when I came in.

"What's happening?" I asked.

"Nothing Beti, go do your homework."

But if it was nothing, why were we no longer allowed to play in the road? Why were we taken and collected from school now, my Paapa rotating with Dani's Father?

One morning we went to pick Dani up for school. She wasn't there. No-one was. Everything was locked up. My parents didn't seem surprised.

"Don't worry Urmila, they've probably gone on holiday." Instinct told me this wasn't true, Dani wouldn't go away without telling me. She always told me even if she only went to visit her nani and nana in Chamba and came back with peanut brittle and bangles to share.

People started leaving. They collected what they could on carts, carrying suitcases and bags threading out of the village like a line of ants. Where were Dani and Zubin? Where was everyone going?

A group of relatives and neighbours collected at our house. I heard raised voices behind the closed door:

"We have to leave."

"But where do we go? This is our home."

"Which way do we head?"

I was ushered out to play with the chickens. I wanted to see Dani, talk to her about what was going on that no-one was explaining. My Chachcha came outside for a cigarette.

"Why the sad face Urmila?" he asked.

"She's missing Dani from across the road," Mama told him, coming out to give me a banana, smiling at me in her sympathetic way.

"She was Muslim, no? No more playing with Muslim girls."

"Nahim Kabir, they're children. Stop!" Mother was really annoyed.

My uncle shrugged and spat a glistening globule onto the dusty yard. "It's happening soon enough."

"What's happening?" I asked.

"Enough!" Mother said, ushering him inside.

That evening my parents told me to choose a favourite toy or book. We were leaving the next day to visit dadi and daadaa in Sikkim. I chose a wooden doll painted in a red sari who housed smaller identical dolls inside. With this doll I could take a whole family. We woke at sunrise and made our way to the train station. My parents carried suitcases and I had a bag with schoolbooks, a couple changes of clothes and my doll.

"What about the chickens, Mata?"

"Beti, we can't carry them. We have a long journey."

"No, I can't leave Jamilah and Durga! I'll carry them." Tears rolled down my face and under my chin, dropping into the scratched dirt next to the chicken pen.

"Shush. Come on, jaldee. We have to go."

I cried without making a noise, not wanting to make my Father angry. My head ached from the effort. Why was everything changing? We trudged onto the road out of the village. There were many people around despite the light still being hazy. Some carried babies, bags, pans, rice; a woman helped an elderly man making slow painful progress. It was like a festival day, only no-one was celebrating – people looked fearful and drained. There was a hush despite the number of people travelling. Everyone seemed to be headed the same way.

After an hour, with many stops to rest and change cases into the other hand, we were twenty yards from the station when there was a shuddering scream, sobbing, people shouting, running in the opposite direction.

"Wait under that tree," my Father instructed. Although my Mother begged him not to go, he hurried to see what was going on. He returned minutes later looking ashen. "We must get away from here now. There's no way out from the station." He started walking fast, the heavy case banging his legs, almost tripping.

"What is it?"

"People—bodies. I saw a boy—a baby. It was Zubin..."

Overview

Jessica McCarthy

The thrust of the rocket engine forced Jason back into the impact couch behind him. He closed his eyes as he tried not to think about the fact that he was riding what was essentially a controlled chemical explosion inside a tin can into space. An extremely high-tech tin can that had undergone a great deal of testing and evaluation, and a very well-controlled explosion, but a tin can and an explosion nonetheless.

The rocket rose higher into the atmosphere, arcing along its pre-programmed trajectory. The force on Jason lessened, and he opened his eyes. At this stage in the journey, there was nothing he could do other than look at the displays and the readouts that told him everything was fine and working according to plan. He took a deep, gulping breath as he tried to convince himself that he was fine, that everything was safe, whilst simultaneously ignoring the fact that if his capsule depressurised at this point, despite still being within the atmosphere and despite being strapped in, he would be sucked out of the tin can and would not survive long enough to be concerned about the eventual impact.

A sudden jolt in the structure of the rocket unnerved Jason, convincing him that it was coming apart around him, before one of the displays helpfully reminded him that it was just the first stage of the craft being jettisoned and the engines of the second kicking in. Jason took another deep breath, slightly less gulping than before, and tried to remember some of the meditation exercises that he had practised prior to lift-off, but found that his current situation rendered most of them impossible to put into practice, and his mental state rendered the remainder useless.

The engines cut out and the second stage fell away, and Jason suddenly found his body pushing against the restraining straps that held him in place. A quick glance at one of the nearby displays confirmed his thoughts; he was in space. Wanting a more concrete demonstration of what he already knew in the abstract to be true, he reached for a nearby touch pen, pulling it loose from the Velcro binding that held it to the side of his chair. He held it up before him and released it. Instead of falling, the pen continued to float in the air before him. Jason could have laughed if his stomach wasn't still tied up in knots from the nerves of the launch.

A faint rumble from behind interrupted Jason as the pen floated past his head and impacted the couch beside him. The engines of the final stage had kicked in, guiding Jason towards his final destination. It was at this moment, more than any other, that Jason wished the designers of the spacecraft had thought to include windows somewhere in the cockpit so he could see where he was going. He knew, academically, that such windows would be a structural weakness, but that didn't stop him from wanting to be able to see out of his craft.

The main screen in front of Jason changed to show a video feed from the camera mounted to the nose of the craft. The screen displayed a large white station, adorned with spindly antennae and glittering solar panels, hanging silently in the endless black void of space. The ship's computer helpfully highlighted the docking port that Jason was aiming for. He reached out and took hold of the joystick that he would use to guide himself the rest of the way. Focusing hard, Jason was vaguely aware that his tongue had snuck out of his mouth and was pressed against his upper lip in the way that it so often did when he was concentrating on something. Ignoring it, he instead concentrated on making the tiny, precise adjustments that were needed to mate his ship with the port on the station, almost not daring to breathe in case an exhalation of air at an inopportune moment would be enough to send him off course, or worse – crashing into the station.

After what felt to Jason like hours, but was surely less than a minute, he felt the reassuring clunk of the station's docking port connecting with its counterpart on his craft, and moments later, the displays around him lit up in a reassuring green, confirming that the connection was solid and safe. Finally releasing the breath that he had been holding on to in a sigh of relief, Jason let go of the joystick and slumped back into his chair. Unbuckling himself from the restraints, he made his way past the now retracted displays towards the airlock.

On the other side of the airlock was a module that looked like a long white hallway, barely wide enough for two people to pass in; the walls covered in lockers and equipment. It nonetheless felt impossibly spacious compared to the cramped confines of the capsule which Jason had just exited. Pulling on the straps on the walls, Jason slowly and carefully floated along the module towards a long, narrow window in one of the sides. Upon reaching it, he steeled himself before looking out and taking in the sight before him.

His first, unaided, view of space was slightly disappointing. The vista was mostly black, with a scattering of stars around the edges, but as he watched, the orbital motion of the station brought a thin blue crescent into Jason's view, and the crescent only continued to grow. As Jason watched, he began to make out the outlines of continents, until eventually the blue and green filled the entirety of the disk – and he found himself looking down upon the full Earth. It was strange, he realised, he could pick out the different continents, and he knew where the different countries were. He could point to the United States, or to Russia, or Brazil, but he couldn't tell where the border between China and India lay. There were no convenient lines present on the Earth before him to tell him exactly which parts of the planet belonged to which group of humans. Jason suddenly felt very small and a sense of awe, as he realised that, from up here, there were no borders.

A Chicken in the Oven

Grace Amui

Ten more minutes. That's all Valerie wants. Driving on the A41 motorway is rarely a problem for her – no matter the number of cars that fill it on a Saturday afternoon – except when she's late.

Valerie had ironed Rachel's floral violet dress as her little girl showered, ensuring her daughter could slip the clothes on within a matter of three minutes and twenty-nine seconds. The scent of success emanated from Valerie's hair, a blend of coconut conditioner and thick aloe gel that had slicked her afro into a tight bun. She had hoovered the floor to such an extent the dust had disappeared. She'd dried and stacked the dirty dishes from yesterday's Uber Eats delivery before Rachel could arise and shine.

According to the Mum Awards, today, Valerie was at the top of her game, rising over every hurdle – until Elizabeth Odoï's name announced itself as three letters on her phone screen, ripping Valerie's medal from her grasp.

Mum.

"Valerie, where are you?" Her mother's high voice rang like an alarm.

"Morning, ma. Just finished cleaning, still at home." Valerie watched Rachel carefully as she sat in her purple gown. No cereal, no dust: no stains would touch that thing.

"Cleaning? Well done...it's your sister's engagement today." Mum said, clearly disregarding that she told Valerie yesterday, and on numerous days in the past month. "What are you bringing Dianne's guests?"

"The rice, like you asked. We finished it this morning." Valerie smiled through the phone, grinning at the finished product glistening in the pot.

"Ah, rice." Mum paused briefly. "With chicken?"

"...Chicken? I'm sure someone will make that for Dianne's vegetarian boyfriend." Valerie replied, not wanting to mention that she avoided eating the meat in her freezer nowadays. From Valerie's perspective, her sister's engagement was meant to be a surprise, and lacking meat on the menu could add to the thrill.

Mum never asked for chicken – and neither did Valerie.

The ten minutes lead her here, turning her Nissan Qashqai into the familiar Hampstead neighbourhood. The sun beams, evidently preferring parts of London where a siren doesn't sound every hour. Unlike Valerie's Colindale estate, where she covers her blue Nissan to avoid tempting dodgy criminals. Here, all vehicles shine brightly like actors in the spotlight. Valerie isn't superficial, but she knows that at least an eight is present on the licence plates of her sister's entire neighbourhood, emphasising that these vehicles were not purchased before 2018.

Two years after her little girl was born.

"Look," Rachel squeals, subtly biting her nails, "Mummy, those balloons are humongous!" The seven-year-old's voice amplifies in the closed space.

Valerie swerves into Hampstead Reach's gated community. Instead of the typical two inflatables stand four clusters leading to the apartment building, as though Dianne and her ready-to-propose boyfriend did not own one flat, but all six inside.

"There must be millions of balloons!" Rachel unbuckles her seatbelt as the car meets a safe halt.

"Millions of pounds." Valerie says, glad that her voice comes out too quietly for her little girl, running to the front door, to notice. Especially glad that her voice doesn't reach the familiar frame strolling through the door. Uncle Bernard and his latest mistress walk out, practically intertwined with each other. He pauses, shaking his ringed hand with Rachel's, the unnamed lady bouncing every bit and bob like a slinky as she moves.

"Rachel! Ah, look at how you've grown." His accent merges with Accra and Atlanta. Valerie is sure he's only been to the States for a flight stopover, but she rarely spends enough time with him to care where Bernard's accent stems from.

Rachel grins, performing amusement for the burly uncle chuckling at his peculiar jokes about children these days. Spoilt children in London, kids who never experienced the cane at school, youngsters who—

"Here." Like two entrepreneurs, Uncle Bernard's same hand slips a twenty-pound note into his great-niece's palm. "Get yourself some hot chocolate."

Hot chocolate from where? Harrods?

Valerie can't avoid winking at Rachel as her mother's brother stalks away with his bouncing lady. Growing up, Valerie had her fair share of transactions with Uncle Bernard, despite her mother's usual request for her brother to stop.

Speaking of mothers, Valerie has less than a breath to encounter hers as door six opens. The flat door spills over with even more sparkling balloons, floating with helium rather than the standard carbon dioxide Valerie uses when blowing those for herself. Mum stands with a phone to her ear, like a bouncer blocking Dianne's corridor.

"I am just so, so grateful to God for my firstborn, about to be engaged – Valerie! What is this? You are late."

Just by a few minutes.

"Afternoon, ma. The rice is in the car. Your chicken needs to be cooked, but I followed Grandma Hilda's recipe. I can't believe you asked me today—"

"Ah, is that my granny gal, granny daughter? Look at you, stronger each week we meet!" As always, her mother and, now-rich, daughter begin dancing to the Highlife rhythm softly playing from the living room. An unspoken conversation of bliss bursts between them, leaving Valerie to bolt to the kitchen at the sound of the doorbell, only to bump into her worst nightmare.

A gathering of women squawking at one another with freshly cooked containers of fish and sweet boffrot and beef, and surprisingly...no chicken.

Mother's entourage.

Valerie freezes, more than a metre in, staring at clashing pots and bright dresses. Just like in the past, she stands stuck to the cream-tiled floor. Their backs face her, but their voices fling around the room.

"Where's the spatula?" Aunty Janice leads the flock in conversation.

"Did you not bring one?"

"Ah. Elizabeth's daughter is getting engaged to a Ghanaian doctor: that's big money!"

"She's done much better than the other one. The vegetarian."

"Did you bring chicken? No chicken? We better get—"

A deer in headlights. A hen before the farmer. In a moment, the Highlife beat falls silent. Valerie's heart drops to her stomach. Auntie Janice, an auntie by respect – not blood – turns from the kitchen counter. Her pencilled eyebrow cocks up as her gaze lands upon the uncooked bird carried in Valerie's hands, in front of Valerie's torso. Almost instinctively, the busy entourage turns too, eyeing the chicken with piercing looks.

It's the same look she received seven years ago.

Friday Nights at Wetherspoons: "I don't miss him"

Natasha Stewart

*Hospital: the clock skipped a tick
and struck thirteen; seconds and decades;
a single blink by milky eyes.*

*The flick of a scalpel and the 'Y'.
Why? He peers at the cold mortuary.
"Go home," the doctor said.*

*His corpse stood up. A late night,
such politeness breaks the mind.
A dead man shrugged and*

*with a wink, kissed ear lobes
and coccyges. Guinness and
pick-up lines and stolen scrubs.*

*A reverse-strip tease. He twerked
his peach dimpled bum. My boyfriend
always loved his ladies.*

The clock struck twelve. A little fantasy
was broken. My grief

is the same to memory as its presence
is to pictures: brown bruises and blank
like one-night stands and beer and my
anxiety-induced dissociation.
"Scot-free! Bloody cut him up—" like a doctor.

 I don't miss him.

Sometimes

Tamsyn Marie Down

Sometimes the shush and the hush gets
Too much
When your feelings are raging
No point in then caging them in
Just to fit in
To someone else's notion
Of what is outspoken.

Sometimes you're broken
Hiding
Instead of confiding the fears
Holding you down
Edging your reasoning
Just to blend in
To someone else's notion
Of what is commotion.

Share your pattern
With pride
Put to the side:
the doubters, the frowners
the set-in stone downers

Confound expectation.
Grow with rejection.

What you will find is the call to be kind.
Begin from within
To sow the seed
That you only need to
Believe in yourself to
Achieve.

Let's meet in the mind
Being one of a kind
Kind to each other,
to brother, to sister.
Embrace each face.
Displace the rat race.
Replace with grace.

Seeing beyond borders,
Round corners,
Finding horizons...
Beginnings.
Winning hearts,
Not tearing apart.

Sometimes the time to change is
Now.
To absolve, resolve,
Evolve
Stronger.
Together as one.
One of a kind.
One who is kind.

Eternal Sunshine

Sophie Nambufu

Clean slate, a spotless mind and a life without you now undefined.
I could get used to this I tell myself three times a day and night.
The truth is I hope there's an invisible string between us where love lingers and not all hope of reconciliation is lost.
An eternal optimist they call me. I'm quite fond of the nickname actually even if it's making a mockery of me at times. *Never afraid of being wrong twice.*
I simply cannot let overthinking be the architect of my downfall nor the opinions of others.
Neither can I waste time pondering at the borders leading me back to your whereabouts, longing for your return.
I've found a place for you to seek refuge in my heart and in my prayers, and if time is kind enough, maybe we'll be able to reflect on times with one another not so distant upon remembrance.

I am the Borderless

Alex Ayling-Moores

THE JAR

The jar sits under stuffy air vents upon a table as grey as Berlin Wall brick.
 Clouds within tumble rebelliously. Against the glass. Against themselves.

AGENT LEAR NOEL

Buttocks still fidgeting within the tight constrictions of the plastic chair, wind builds up in Agent Noel's bubble gut and releases squeakily: a whoopee cushion fart. He chuckles to himself (and to the jar?), and scratch, scratch, scratches fingernails through brittle chin stubble.
 The jar says nothing.
 He's kept watch on the jar (and its brewy brooding) for the past hour, sat at the desk, blowing cigarette puffs toward it: teasing, provoking, studying.
 Noel takes another drag and – alone – lets the ashy smoke cloak around the translucent boundaries of his silent opponent. As his puffs slink up into the air vents and dissipate, Noel wonders if any of the

black smoke has slipped into the jar, undetected. An alien invasion.

What would happen if it did? Would it spoil what lurked inside?

The door behind him beeps and whines ajar. Dr. Hendrix leans against it. She's looking paler than usual. Phantom white. Still expressionless though. Always difficult to read.

"The room is ready." She says. "If you want to finish your cigarette outside..."

Noel asks where the room is. Dr. Hendrix tells him she'll escort him there herself.

The jar says nothing.

DR. ALICE HENDRIX

"Two secs..." Agent Noel calls out. He's struggling to keep up. "I'm almost done."

The balding man's ciggy stench-musk clings to the air, saturating it, clogging it the same way it clogs up Alice's nostrils. Perfumed fingers pressed against her nose do little to restrict the access. Then: phew! She hears him flick the butt of his last drag into a dustbin a few paces back.

Yet still it lingers. The smell: smokey, homely.

It follows. Dragging.

Dragging her yonder to dragging hours lounging at Jasper and Emelda's almost a decade back, the ashtray brimming, her arms hugged against a cushion as the married lovebirds beside her debate the relevance of Hume in contemporary understandings of the subconscious, soon both disputing the importance of AI to future generations.

"The modern mind," Jasper had remarked slyly, "has forgotten two things: that it's not so modern, and it isn't just a mind. Wet meat bouncing around old skulls. We're more than bright screens and invisible wires. We're more than just air..."

Back then, Alice was their surrogate child. Or perhaps that's just how she had always felt.

To them, she'd probably been more of a niece. She adored them. She still adores them. She read every paper that Jasper and Emelda published. She even helped proof one or two of the later ones. Charming, eccentric, their theories reflected their character, their relationship: militantly whimsical. And yet despite all the obscure convolution and esoteric pontifications was a pure, simple root:

Consciousness is chemical.

Therefore it wasn't the Psychotherapists, nor the Neuroscientists who would colonise the territories of human consciousness. It was the Chemists. They were the ones who were destined to plant their flags upon that great discovery.

Jasper and Emelda had made it their lives work. Their baby.

But then last year Jasper died. Stolen away. A car accident. On slippery roads he collided with a drunk driver. The night it happened Emelda said she had died too. She'd weeped it down the phone: "I want to be gone, forever..."

Endlessly Emedla and Jasper had ruminated on their holy grail hypothesis, even given it their own name: 'Solipsistic Sublimation'. The theory went that if you could extract consciousness itself from the brain and modify it into a gas then – at its core – you would've proven the alchemy of sentience. Thus you could then begin to understand its mysteries in a far more physical sense; rather than merely referencing a bunch of expensive x-rays and surrealist guesstimates, you could actually touch another's identity. Even breathe it in.

And it seems that after Jasper's death – in grief – Emelda figured out how to do it.

Because she did it to herself.

"Dr. Hendrix!" A member of the Prep-Team stares at her through biohazard gear. "We're ready to finalise preparations when you are."

Alice nods. She turns, sees Agent Noel held back by an intruder: Frances Upward.

The Home Secretary knows she isn't allowed down here. Despite her party's hard line on immigration sloganed as Legal Access Applies To All, she clearly doesn't believe the sentiment has a whiff of relevance to herself.

(THE RIGHT HONOURABLE) FRANCES UPWARD

Her husband doesn't know she's here. Not even her advisors. Agent Noel, the doctor, no one wants her to be here. She doesn't want to be here either. But Frances must be loud, she must be abrasive, she must be brave, for her daughter. Kathy. The spoilt brat.

Hot rivulets soak her fingertips, slipping down in the crevices of her knuckles with no hope of flowering the dry cracks (she's spent far more on lotions than she'd ever care to admit).

"This all must be very stressful," Dr. Hendrix says.

"It's just the corridor lights," Frances snaps. "I'm fine."

That's what it is. Not her nerves.

Although most would be sweating buckets over this, wouldn't they?

It was bad enough when the Home Secretary thought her daughter's disappearance was just down to flattery. Flattery from a bunch of so-called Anarchists staunchly opposed to Frances' own immigration policies. But a lot's happened since then. Tragedy snowballs quickly.

Now the woman finds herself in a secret bunker hidden beneath Hadrian's Wall – a stuffy old bunker not used since Churchill's premiership – because she's been told her daughter has been trapped in a jar...trapped in a jar!? Yes. Trapped. In. A. Jar.

How confusing! How stressful! And not one person has even offered her a cup of tea.

Just complaints. Why are you here? Who let you in? Why aren't you leaving?

"This is restricted access," Dr. Hendrix reminds her. "If you don't go now I'll have you escorted out. You're not allowed—"

Frances doesn't care. She butts through the door anyway, calling out to her daughter, "Kathy! Kathy!? Mummy's here, darling! You're alright now."

But her daughter is nowhere to be seen...

At this point Frances can hear Agent Noel and Dr. Hendrix muttering in the corner.

"She'll be less hassle this way..." Noel suggests.

A few tense minutes later, and Dr. Hendrix is explaining the preparations to Frances.

From the control room they're standing in, they look through into another. The doctor relates it to an anechoic chamber. Frances doesn't know what that is. So the doctor defines it: a room of pure isolation of sound. Nothing can be echoed or reflected within it.

"I see," Frances says, her eyes narrowing as if she's spotted a gazelle in the Serengeti, gritting her teeth with a jackhammer bite, strong enough to pierce a fat neck and drag a fresh carcass back to her young. "Go on..."

"Well," Dr. Hendrix continues, "this room is the same, but with gases. Right now my team is putting the glass jar safely inside the control room. After that they shall leave and we will attempt communication with whatever lives inside."

"And how will you do that?" Frances is perplexed; scared? No... never scared.

"Let us show you." Dr. Hendrix places her hand on Frances' shoulder.

The Home Secretary shoves it off. The process begins:

With the chamber completely sealed, a mechanical grabber is activated. Slow and measured, the device whirrs as it locates the lid of the jar and opens it. At this point the gas inside – a chorus of saturated colours – floats upward and then erratic as if trying to orient itself.

This pacing soon slows, at which point another mechanical device starts up: the microphone. It is pointed carefully at the gas. Frances watches with clenched fists. She aches to speak to her daughter, but only Dr. Hendrix is allowed to use the microphone.

Agent Noel leaves the room to light up another cigarette.

The doctor says, "...Hello?"

THE BORDERLESS

"Youcannotcageus," the gas speaks in tutti, "wearefreefromallborders nowandforever," many voices as one: a choir singing from the same hymn sheet. Uncompromising unison.

It continues:

"Wearefreefromyourculturaltyranny!weareanarchisminarcanate beyondanyideology!wearebiologicallynomadicfreetoroameverywhere! IisWe!WeareI!" Yet a solitary voice cuts through the voice-chord now: "Motheristhatyou?ithinkicanseeyou?" It is weaker than the rest.

"Imsosorry!pleaseforgiveme!Ididntunderstandwhat—" the voice is soon cut off.

"Iarecompletelyequalandfreetovoiceouridentitytogetherwithoutthe constraintsofoligarchs."

Another voice now cuts through. "Theseprotestersareinsane." Only Dr. Hendrix recognises the voice. She sobs at its sound. "Theyarewellmeaningbutstupidandtheyhaveutterlyappropriated—" The other voices are trying to interrupt, "—mineandjasperslifeswork —" The voice is becoming muffled. "Ijustwantedtobeleftalone ijustwantedtobeatpeace," the other voices return, cacophonous:

"IAMTHEBORDERLESS!" Then all of it says it again, louder, "IAMTHEBORDERLESS!"

Some of it in triumph, some of it in turmoil, one of it in regret.

13.

Grace Amui

You remember that non-school uniform day.
Sat solo on McDonald's leather, imprinted on by many students like you.
You remember, glistening green at thirteen.
Glasses handpicked in *Claire's accessories*, unprescribed, yet suiting your plaits.

You recall the warmth.
As Mr. Watson mentioned your style.
You recall the neon.
As *she* scowled at your smile.
Green glasses brighter than the sizzling sun outside.

You retell this moment.
In your head alone. Your oblivious friends cued for coated chicken.
You retell this no more.
How the hawk glared at you. Like prey on predator. Don't be stricken.

You re-used it: never again.
Still stuffed in the corner, squashed by other neglected treasures.
"Why the glasses, though?"
You returned to a blazer all school kids submitted to.

Loving at opposite ends of the day

Helen Williams

As her day draws to a close
She sinks gratefully into the sheets
And thinks of her eldest
Spinning on a stage
Sparkling at this very moment
As she, herself, drifts
Into oblivion.
And she thinks of her middle child
Lighting up another stage
With his bird's-eye view
From the top of an auditorium
Or pumping sound into a club.
Their working days have hardly begun
As hers dissolves into darkness.
She switches off the lamp
And raises her arms
For the goodnight hug
From the insomniac adolescent
The youngest,
Who will toss and turn for hours
Until she drags her into the new dawn
Tomorrow...while the others drop

Exhausted into unfamiliar beds
Wherever they've landed
On this leg
Of their tour
Of the 21st Century.

Sweet Buns

Emma Lindsey

It's not that *I* mind, it's other people. Like Carol. She and soporific hubby, Pete, are coming over this Sunday for lunch. Not sure if they're bringing the boys. God, I hope not. Last time the little sods managed to find cat shit in the garden and trod it all over the house, including into my new Axminster triple twist carpet. It was hell to get out, had to use a toothbrush in the end. Ruined of course. I've put a coffee table over the rough patch, but you know when you know it's there?

But worse than having them over, what I'm dreading is the "How did you meet?" question. Carol hasn't asked yet, but I know my little sister, and she's been flying low for a while, so that bomb's about to drop. Not that I actually give a toss, mind you. I'm used to it now. The narrow-eyed looks we get from people, trying to work us out. Doesn't help Tomek can't keep his hands or his lips off me. You can see the question in their eyes. On account of him looking like a Strip-o-Gram, without the oil, and me, looking, well, a bit like his mum, or maybe an aunt. That's if I didn't make an effort. One thing with a younger man, you've got to keep your end up. Luckily, I used to teach PE, and it's amazing what a bit of collagen in the right place does, along with a monthly Brazilian.

Anyway. Whatever Carol comes out with – last time it was how well their stocks were performing, and whether to buy a villa in Portugal or a chalet in Chamonix – Tomek will be fine. Smiling, gorgeous, never a bad word to say about anyone – not that I can understand anyway. It's one of the reasons he caught my eye during the refurb. He's a 'happy-go-lucky chappy', as my Uncle Bob would say.

When I got my loft done, Tomek was one of the builders.

I noticed he never kept his shirt on long. Though to be fair, it *was* during the heatwave. Better than a *Coke* advert. Next time I saw him, he was on a roof in the next road. I was on my way back from teaching Zumba. He recognised me, as it happens; shouted down, I looked up and Boom! Chakalaka!

Turned out it was his great big van parked in front of my driveway. By sheer coincidence, my fuse box was sparking. He soon sorted that; gave him a smoked salmon roll and it didn't take long before it was more than his van that was parked up.

It's been nearly a year now. His English isn't great, but we understand each other in the ways that matter. I've never known muscles like it. Sculpted granite. Said he likes the taste of a woman. Got a big appetite. And staying power? He could go on for the whole EU, never mind Poland. Not like my ex, John, the two-minute no wonder.

He's 38, hands like shovels, with the fingers of a pianist. He makes soup with pork dumplings and lovely sweet buns. Sometimes, to be honest it's a lot more than I can chew, but I'm not about to look this gift horse in the mouth. He's from a place called Zakopane. It looks beautiful. Wants to take me there, to meet his family but I'm not sure. At this stage of the game – 72 in August – I'm not looking for a new mother-in-law, or another walk down the aisle.

A Walking Metaphor

Damian R. Laprus

He was the oddest of the bunch. A man who enjoyed spicing himself up with cheap sauvignon and feminine perfume, preferably citrusy. Fresh, but too cliché for a man of his status. He was the kind who conceptualised himself on purpose, ironically. The irony itself poured out of his mouth quite often. Cynical acid, wrapped in a Southern European accent. He was the type to find profound meaning in everything, but that one night…that one bloody night he couldn't find a plausible explanation for his misery.

He was drinking in a pub. His intensity frightened both the staff and the people around him. He had been drinking for hours, motionlessly staring at the wall ahead of him. He looked dead, although his cheeks were as red as two bloody rubies. There was madness in his eyes. Nobody was brave enough to make eye contact. No one dared to tell him off.

"Another bottle—" he roared suddenly.

The barman was startled. His goosebumps visible through his white shirt.

"We…we are no longer serving, sir."

The gentleman twisted his torso slowly. He impaled the bartender with his pupils, sharp as two knives, corroded by grief and ethanol. The bartender didn't waste any more time and took out a random bottle from the bar and rolled it flat in the gentleman's direction. He caught the bottle, bit the cap off and spat it out on the floor. Took six massive gulps. The booze dripped over his face, then down his neck and shirt. He stood up shortly after.

He opened his mouth widely. One would have expected him to say something powerful or even scary. The man had a dark aura but apparently an even darker gut. He let out one of the gnarliest farts one could squeeze out of their butt. He left the pub shortly after, limping a bit.

Afterwards, he roamed around the city. He dragged himself helplessly through the streets, imitating the wind, changing his pace and directions abruptly. People tried to ignore him, yet curiosity lifted their noses from their smartphones when he passed by. The aroma he carried combined with a blank stare in his eye made people walk around him. He stopped right outside a bookshop. He processed what he saw for a second, then slammed the door open and entered.

He marched through the aisles, knowing exactly where to go. He knew that place well. He stopped at the poetry aisle. The shelves were full of different fonts and colours. He stared at one book, particularly angry. He picked up two copies and gripped them roughly.

By the time he even got to the cashier, the lady working the till was suspiciously scoping him out. He threw the books on the counter and leaned forward.

"Sixteen pounds, please." She instinctively took a step back.

He tossed her a twenty – "Keep the change." Then stared inside her brain, through the nostrils. She was a bit intimidated but after a while, her facial expression changed from concerned to excited.

"Wait...aren't you that famous poet?!"

"*Poet?*" He brutally mocked her accent.

She looked at him confused. "Author of the book...that you're buying."

"You flatter me, lady. I am not as handsome as that guy."

She examined him closely. "How do you maintain yourself in such a manner?"

"I draw borders. Boundaries!" He giggled "Th-thank you." He smiled wide. His two front teeth were missing. She jumped back. He left the place shortly after, laughing a bit.

A writer is a bizarre creature. Able to transform alcohol into books. In his case, the books were not a part of creation but destruction. He wandered aimlessly through the city's gloomy alleyways, looking for a secluded place.

He went down an alley. He pressed his back onto a cold, brick wall. It was melting his spine with shivers, yet he remained still. After a while, he peeked to check one last time. Nobody was after him. That place was a rogue apartment, hidden away between two huge walnut trees. It was abandoned, as the broken windows and lack of cars in the driveway indicated. That's where it happened.

He took out a lighter and set the first few pages on fire. The fire burned him, so he dropped the book in an instant. The second copy he laid on the ground trying to set each page on fire individually. He did that seeing the first one, cold and in the mud… barely touched by the flame.

He kicked one of the copies and screamed. "Why won't you just burn?!" He dropped to his knees. He tried to cover the flame within the palm of his hand and then directed it into the paper. Finally, the fire spread.

He grinned, inhaling the smoke. Stretching his arms wide, he tilted his chin upward, a silent yearning coursing through him. A desire to be consumed, to kindle a blaze within. A longing for self-immolation, an internal detonation. His body convulsed, a symphony of spasms taking hold. Laughter, once vibrant, now echoed with desperation, bordering on the brink of mania. Slowly, he descended to the gritty ground beneath him. The parchment was gone and with it, his immortality.

"Spare me a fag, will ya?" An old man's voice penetrated the darkness of the sketchy corner.

Hearing it, the poet stood up rapidly. He wiped the tears from his face. While turning back he reached into his pocket.

An ancient man stood before him. A worm who shed six dozen times already, gliding through the earth without any purpose. He wore a thin, lime tracksuit stretched out to the limit. His eyebrows hung low.

The poet pulled out two cigarettes from his jacket. He apologetically bowed and gave one to the homeless old man.

"Lighter?" The homeless man answered nonchalantly.

The poet turned and came up to the book that was still burning. He crouched and lit the cigarettes from his burning soul. He gave it to the old man, again.

"Won't you even bother to speak to me?"

"There are no words left in me, old man. Only spite. So, I prefer to stay quiet. Out of respect."

The poet stabbed the man with a look, his drunken gaze on the old man before turning away, but the man grabbed his shoulder.

"You need to put the fire out!" he stated aggressively. "Otherwise, it will spread"

"Let it spread," the poet snarled.

The old man smirked. "It surely does sound revolutionary...but is your immortality worth burning?"

The poet couldn't contain his smile. He was shocked that the man recognised him.

"So, you know who I am?"

"Everyone in this Goddamn city knows who you are! You were a poster boy for all the tabloids. Look at you now!"

The passionate response stunned the poet. "What do you see now?" he giggled sarcastically.

"A soul shattered by the loss of his beloved wife. A man in profound pain, grappling with aching emotions. To navigate the void left by his loss, he finds solace in misguided actions. Aching to obliterate every remnant of his existence, he is bound by the cruel irony that his very visage is immortalised within the pages of the books he once shared with the world."

The poet stood frozen; a visible sting etched upon his countenance in response to the old man's piercing observations. In a suspended moment of silence, he let out a little sigh, a delicate exhale that seemed to carry the weight of a thousand untold stories. "Who are you again?"

"You're suddenly curious, aren't you?" The old man chuckled and walked away.

An un-understandable situation

Jennie Horchover

We can feel so hopeless, so helpless
When it seems like the world is falling apart again
We can feel so angry, so sad
When it seems impossible
That anything anyone does or says can make a difference
As tragedy follows tragedy on the daily news

There is only so much sadness I can bear
And yet
To switch off the news
To stop reading the papers
Seems irresponsible of me
And even a little naïve
Like a child who thinks no one can see them
If they simply cover their own eyes

So I watch, I read, I listen, I learn
I stay informed
But I still don't really understand what is happening
Maybe that's because this is, yet again
An un-understandable situation
And yes, I know that's not a real word

But when countries and leaders
Are allowed to fight over borders
Dividing up land with artificial lines
That aren't real
I think I'm allowed to make up a word

I see people posting their views on social media
And others suggesting that
By not posting your condemnation
You might as well be
Giving your support
And yet I remain silent
Concerned
Confused
Feeling hopeless and helpless
Yet again

The New Normal

Libby Rochester

Borders:
The line that most cross for vacations.
Dreaming of sunny days laid next to a swimming pool or on a hot
    beach.
A new country, a new adventure.
Drinking a cocktail, laughing away as the kids run into the cool water,
the sound of laughter and joy in the air.

But lately, that line is more so for safety.

A lucky few cross the line, breathing the sigh of relief
that comes with leaving the place they once called home,
now rubble, dotted with remains of grenades and bombs.
Soldiers, with guns as big as their forearms, owning the land now.
They were safe here.

Those not so lucky are left with the aftermath,
children's toys, smashed into smithereens, laying in the roads.
Blood dotted across the walls that were once loving homes
that held birthday parties and celebrations.
Kids running from danger, running to survive.
'The new life' does not take away from the pain and sorrow
    experienced just moments before they had to leave.

They were *forced* to leave.

The rush to get everything packed and to move on,
the threat of bombs looming over their heads,
forgetting good memories from just days before in an instant for safety.
Children packing their favourite toys, leaving those that don't secure that special place,
so they have more space to pack other essentials.

Food,
Shelter,
Warm clothes for those cold days that are sure to come.
Living with strangers becomes normal,
hearing blood curdling screams from the injured on the other side of the room.

Borders are what people cross for vacations.

They allow for a sense of freedom in another country,
a break away from the normal.
But lately they have become mostly used for safety.

A terrifying outcome in a world that is reversing backwards.

Let us be lockkeepers

Jennie Horchover

We can put up borders
Create boundaries
Lock ourselves away

Thinking that we're protecting ourselves
From pain and sadness
From the unknown
From difference

Trying to keep ourselves safe
Because we're scared

But how can love and connection get to us
If we're hiding behind
A wall
A mask
A fortress
A heavy impenetrable locked door

Let us rather be lockkeepers
Working together
To open our gates

Inviting others in
Slowly lowering the pressure
Helping us unlock ourselves
And each other

DEDICATIONS

Dear Benjamin

Rowan Reddington

In a maroon suit jacket and loc cap
a Grenfell heart on your lapel, a scrap
of paper for a PowerPoint show,
and a hell of a haul of stories in tow,

you strolled into class. An icon. A rock
star. The ego of a monk. You talked
about playing with Bob Marley's band.
You said that a poem is a song.

And by the way they're not read, they're done.
Then we did our poems at the front
of the class, like showing a lion
your roar in a jar. Mine was so weak

it could barely stand – let alone fight!
let alone dance! – this metaphor-muddling
pseudo-academic abstraction that kinda-rhymed...
Yet *still* you managed to say something wise.

When I heard the news I cried for days
but it's okay: cause you said crying is strong.

And if we can't do your lessons,
we'll do your poems.
We'll do some poems of our own,
we'll sing your song.

Benjamin

Duncan MacDowall

Once he was down but never downtrodden
Too soon was lost but never forgotten
A wordsmith, a rhymer, a teller of tales
A challenge to power; the word that prevails

His voice like a siren: all sky blue and flashing
White power and privilege received a tongue-lashing
No massas, no masters, no chains forged in iron
Nor Empire bonds on the road to Mount Zion

In Handsworth in Stratford in Beijing and Brixton
Animal cruelty: a cause he was fixed-on
No chicken, no beef nor tormented veal
Were ever presented for his evening meal

And children were cherished, and honoured and taught
And martyrs were mentioned; for justice he sought.
As peaked caps go flying in Garrison Lane
And Villa Park crowds are chanting his name

'Benjamin, Benjamin Zephaniah
Benjamin, Benjamin Zephaniah'

Once he was down but never downtrodden
Gone far too soon but never forgotten

A Shoulder Like Yours

Rowan Reddington

That you should leave
just when we need
a shoulder,
like yours.

Just when the wind
howls the trees
& lays the leaves
on the crowded ground,

& that sound—
silence—
rises quiet
through the house.

& the wall flowers listen
& the lightbulbs hold their breath
& nothing happens.
(Again & again.)

But the question leaves its mark:
Where do you turn

*when the person you turn to
is the reason you're turning?*

No prizes for guessing
who we'd like to ask.

For Benjamin

Helen Williams

For the first time, that morning,
You didn't show up for the sun
Or go for a run
So I went off to hide me
In the National Poetry Library
With all of your energy
In the stacks there relaxing
Dedicated to the earth
and the children who care
Your spirit is there
At the Southbank Centre, we
Danced – you set us free
Strangers in synergy
Celebrating your legacy
Your spirit was there
You'd have loved it
That day
You didn't show up for the sun.
On Graduation Day
We, your students, heard you say
I write poems for you
And I hope that one day

You will write poems for me.
Read on and write some.
We'll be neighbourly
In the poetry country
As you said
Think Me
You will be
For ever
And ever
All right
We write
You are
Remembered
After all
Rumour has it
Our destinies are all
(Rumour has it)
De same

List of Contributors

GRACE AMUI recently had her first play, 'This Is Me' performed in Barcelona at age 22. She began writing as a child. Loving the library, she decided to pick up a pen for herself, writing and horridly illustrating short stories about adventures with school friends. Consequently, Grace has had the opportunity to perform her poetry internationally and loves crafting her three P's: prose, poetry and plays. Who knew libraries led to a Theatre and Creative Writing degree?

ALEX AYLING-MOORES is a conjurer of words, music and moving images. He likes painting sunrises at midnight on the floors of lightless basements and is on speaking terms with the Great King Amduscias and all his 29 legions. No one has ever met him. Not even himself. He is very popular. Especially amongst nobodies. You can follow his shenanigans on Instagram @alextellstalltales and @wolfmonkey.official.

AISHA BROWN COLPANI is a recent graduate from the Creative Writing: Novel Pathway master's degree at Brunel. She speaks three languages, and hopes that the Spanish songs on her playlist are helping maintain her fluency in one of them. She enjoys trying new vegetarian recipes, and posts intermittently on @places&posts.

TAMSYN MARIE DOWN is a creative writing undergraduate, a passionate advocate for mental health awareness, and an aspiring writer and poet. Previous published work includes satirical articles in the 'Chatty Chimp', under her pseudonym Lady Tamsyn Marie. As a mature student, life experiences inform her writing. Tamsyn is a proud Mum to three adult children and two black cats. She also enjoys keeping fit, reading and volunteering at Parkrun.

HOLLY GRIEVESON is a writer from Northamptonshire, who studied both BA and MA Creative Writing at Brunel University London. She likes to dabble in prose, poetry and scriptwriting. Holly was taught by Benjamin Zephaniahin her final year of her bachelor's degree and has continued to write poetry ever since.

ALEXIA GUGLIELMI is a half-Filipino and half-Italian writer based in London. She has lived in four countries, speaks two and a half languages, and regularly experiences identity crises as a result. At heart, she is a reader of speculative fiction and romances; her own writing mostly examines colonialism, myth, and the self. You can expect to read all that and more in her current project, which she aims to finish drafting in a year.

SUNDUS HASSAN-NOOLI is a Somali-American writer-poet hailing from the Twin Cities. Her interests are in architecture, sweet treats, and the syncretism of multilingual literature. She writes in all the languages she knows and adores indigenous poetics the most. She has a poetry book coming out and a novel on the way.

JENNIE HORCHOVER lives in North West London with her husband, teenage son and a Bernedoodle. She started writing poetry three years ago after the sudden death of her daughter. She is studying for an MA in Creative Writing at Brunel University and has just started writing her first novel. When not writing or working as a self-employed HR Consultant, Jennie sings in both a barbershop chorus and an acapella octet.

MAHJABEN HUSSAIN is a British-Bangladeshi writer from North London. She has loved writing ever since she hand-wrote her first fantasy book when she was thirteen, because why not? She loves romances and dark fictions that make you think deeper about the world. She is currently discovering the journey of her dystopian debut with a fantasy twist.

HARSHITA KAUSHIK was born and brought up in India. She enjoys writing and reading riveting thrillers, especially the ones that dive deep into human psychology. Can also help you with some beauty tips.

DAMIAN R. LAPRUS, a poet and screenwriter hailing from Siedlce, Poland, embarked on his journey in the UK at the age of nineteen. He pursued his passion by attaining a BA in Theatre and Creative Writing from Brunel University. Amidst adapting to a new language, he showcased his literary prowess by publishing prose and poetry in both English and Polish. Presently, he is immersed in crafting his debut novel, poised for publication in the imminent future.

EMMA LINDSEY graduated from Brunel in 2023 with an MA in Creative Writing (with distinction). An award-winning journalist and former Staff Features writer for The Observer and The Guardian and Daily Mirror, she has contributed numerous freelance articles to The Times, Independent on Sunday, Red magazine and BBC Radio 4. She is also Britain's first black, woman sportswriter for a national newspaper. Her debut novel *Midnight* will be published later this year.

DUNCAN MacDOWALL is a Paddington born mature student on Brunel University's MA course in Creative Writing. He's currently collaborating on a screenplay with Monkey Man writer Paul Angunawela while also working on a debut novel. Duncan has a Birmingham connection as he briefly played professional football for Birmingham City FC in his youth, and is honoured that his tribute poem to a great 'son of the city' is featured here.

JESSICA McCARTHY prefers to live in worlds other than this one and tends to write science fiction or fantasy in order to achieve that. When not writing she is either reading, playing video games, playing Dungeons & Dragons, or building Lego. She hopes you like her work.

MIRA MOOKERJEE is an Indian-English writer and editor based in London. Her creative and journalistic writing has been published in S/He Speaks: Voices of Women and Trans Folx; by the International Human Rights Arts Movement; in WOWZINE; the Journal of Fair Trade; Azeema Magazine; Poetry and Audience, and more. She is particularly interested in literature that focuses on migration, surrealism and shifting identities. She is currently working on her debut novel.

SOPHIE NAMBUFU is a creative writing student based in London, England. She has previously had her work published in Young Writers 2021 Anthology and has co-written a poetry collection titled 'Easier than Lying'. Currently, she enjoys sharing her poetry and is developing her new-found interest in writing young and new adult fiction.

ROWAN REDDINGTON is a poet and tree surgeon living in East London. He's a guitarist, vegan and an environmental activist. He hopes to one day live on a narrowboat with his partner and their hypothetical dog (he believes this will suit both the sensibilities and wages of a poet).

LIBBY ROCHESTER is a 23-year-old Theatre Graduate and Creative Writing Masters Graduate from Brunel University London, who spends her time writing with the hopes of inspiring others. Most days she is either reading or buying more romance novels to add to her mounting 'to be read' list. She is currently writing her own romance and writes poetry in her spare time.

SMRITI SARMA was a dentist once upon a time, but after the plaintive beckoning of the Muse of Creativity became impossible to ignore, she moved from India to London to study Creative Writing. Now a graduate, she loves to read and strives to paint vivid pictures of life and love with her words. Her work has earned her numerous accolades, but she treasures readers' perspectives above all else.

NEELAM SHARMA is a British Indian writer living in London. She works in mental health and is studying for a MA at Brunel University. Her interests are travelling, tennis and of course reading! She has been known to miss her tube stop whilst engrossed in a good book. She was part of a group of writers who created SexPlay, due to be staged 2024/2025. She is working on a novel, a poetry collection and a children's picture book. One of these days she may even finish one of these!

NATASHA STEWART is a confessional poet from South London. Her hobbies include sketching and travel photography. In 2014, she published a poem about chocolate biscuits. Ten years later, she earned an MA in creative writing. Her work explores trauma, dark secrets and literal confessions through free verse text. For Natasha, poems are just another word for diary.

LINDA SWIDENBANK is Welsh, a mix of south and north, and has lived in London almost all her adult life. She attended Brunel University twice, with a forty-year gap in between. For 2024, she's challenged herself to read a work of fiction from every country in the world. So engrossed with the history and culture of the first six on her list, she still has 189 to go. She works part-time in magazine publishing.

HELEN WILLIAMS completed Brunel's MA in Creative Writing in 2023. She was super excited (and somewhat intimidated) when she found out that her lifelong inspiration, Benjamin Zephaniah, was to be her dissertation supervisor. Benjamin's wisdom, humour and guidance enabled her to complete her first Young Adult "action-adventure-murder-mystery-spy novel". Inspired by Benjamin's unwavering belief in following your dreams, Helen is about to begin a PhD in Creative Writing at Brunel.

Acknowledgements

Thank you Benjamin for inspiring so many.

To Bernardine Evaristo, extra special thanks for your advice and for writing our beautiful introduction.

Thank you Max Kinnings and Frazer Lee for your guidance, enthusiasm and support for this project – your help was invaluable.

Thank you Qian Zephaniah for your blessing, and Jodie Hodges for your encouragement.

Thank you Joel Dagostino and Bethan Evans for your invaluable assistance from the very first cover mockup, without which the final design would not have been possible.

To our lovely contributors, *Borderless* would not exist without you. Thank you for sending us your incredible pieces and entrusting us with the honour of publishing them.

Brunel University, thank you for bringing us all together.

And finally, thank you to everyone who helped us along the way. Big or small, your grace, kindness and support kept us going. We hope we've done you proud.

Milton Keynes UK
Ingram Content Group UK Ltd.
UKHW020628090824
446663UK00013B/436